Memoirs of a Spacewoman

MEMOIRS OF A SPACEWOMAN

Naomi Mitchison

A BERKLEY MEDALLION BOOK
published by
BERKLEY PUBLISHING CORPORATION

To Anne McLaren

SBN 425-02345-1

*BERKLEY MEDALLION BOOKS are published by
Berkley Publishing Corporation
200 Madison Avenue
New York, N.Y. 10016*

BERKLEY MEDALLION BOOKS ® TM 757,375

Printed in the United States of America

Berkley Medallion Edition, JUNE, 1973

CHAPTER ONE

I think about my friends and the fathers of my children. I think about my children, but I think less about my four dear normals than I think about Viola. And I think about Ariel. And the other. I wonder sometimes how old I would be if I counted the years of time blackout during exploration. It would be an alarming thought if that kind of thought happened to alarm me. Then I begin to wonder how many more voyages I should undertake, supposing, of course, that I don't get killed. They have asked me to be leader several times, but I do not care for that sort of responsibility. I know I would forget about my expedition if I came on a really interesting communications problem. And one must never forget one's expedition. This expedition we are planning now, back to the butterfly world, I'm not sure I want even to be deputy leader this time. I only want to think about communication problems and what alterations may have taken place since we left.

Sometimes I think of my life in terms of time: my own time and the very different times of other people. And sometimes I think of it in terms of moral problems. We Terrans have always had moral problems, or so the back-time-explorers tell us. Many other forms of conscious life have not been bothered that way. Yet there are some worlds which have had an even more complicated moral set-up than we have, especially when there is not one, but two or more, dominant species. Perhaps we're well out of that.

The more we explore, the more problems meet us. Yet would we have it otherwise? I think not. Humans were beginning to run out of serious moral problems about the time that space exploration really got going. The mid-twentieth century had been full of them, but when most of them had proved to be quite easily soluble—given, of course, that solution really was desired—there was quite a danger of moral boredom. Well, we can't say that now!

Naturally, we did not realise at once that time blackout was going to make difficulties. It took a few major scandals to clear that up, and after all the Terran incest taboo has a quite sensible biological basis. Nowadays the parent-child relationship is rather strictly organised, so that we are not tempted to fall in love with our sons, however much they have grown up during our time blackouts; sometimes, I feel, we get over-conditioned, so that we are not even normally attracted to them in an affectionate way. I should hate that to happen to me! But of course there are also one's friends' sons.

However, I know as well as the rest that one shouldn't let oneself be attracted, and at least all my children's fathers were in my own age group or older. One ought to leave the young alone. How many times I've said that to myself! And usually, I will say, acted on it.

Still, that's the least of the problems, for it is strictly Terran, although naturally in other worlds with a comparable socio-sexual organisation, the same thing arises. It just doesn't happen on Mars, Vly tells me, and that makes sense. Far more of our today's problems are connected with interference. Before the codifying of rules for space explorers, there were constant examples of deliberate interference with other life, almost always ending disastrously and making communication less easy for several generations. It is still one's major temptation and that is why the penalty is irrevocable: to be returned to earth or whatever one's planet may be and never, any more, to be an explorer. To be bound to time. And how often, still, the penalty has to be employed. I have been near enough to it myself. Just as I have been very near to having the whole stability of my personality altered and shattered in an irreversible way.

Naturally, the young are impatient. I know I was. The tides of curiosity are rising, and one becomes pressingly aware of all the galaxies. Even when one realises that it will take years to learn to communicate, one longs all the same to be off. It's not for nothing that most of the workable short-cutting circuits, as well as almost all the unworkable ones, were discovered by the under-thirties. Some of them indeed have been the work of men and women who realised that their genetic make-up was such that communication would always be difficult. Knowledge of other sciences can be borrowed or shared, but communication is essential. And meanwhile there are the other worlds waiting.

One reads and watches, one steeps oneself in 3D and 4D; one practises detachment in the face of apparently disgusting and horrible events; one practises taking bizarre points of view. And one is told about time blackout. It was my mother who told me. She was just back from a voyage, and I had suddenly realised that, although I had been growing up and feeling in every cell of my body the marvellous, beautiful sweep of the Terran seasons, the Arctic spring, the flickering lightning of the monsoons, the crash of the west Atlantic hurricanes, yet she seemed unchanged. As a child I had accepted this without bothering: there are stable older people in one's life, and one's own loved group, with whom one first experiments in sex play and verse and painting. For me and my friends, parents and grandparents came and went, though occasionally one would reach an age where he or she decided to give up exploration and settle back into time. Then, fairly soon, they would be dead. Or sometimes there might be parents who were not explorers, but mainly, for example, administrators, though they too might fairly often go long distances and experience time blackout. But not as a matter of course. They began to look old; my mother never did.

We are all able to love our parents. Our conflicts with older people do not involve them, because they just aren't there to be reacted against. We react quite enough against the Terran non-explorers, poor things; not that they think of themselves in that light. And I realised, of course, that my mother had given me a year of her life, stabilising me, the customary slow-motion year which, to speak the complete truth, I have always enjoyed myself, even though it is a temporary surrender to time. There are moments, aren't there, when surrender is delicious, even to that old enemy.

So my mother explained it all, and various things which I had read and not understood came into focus. Time blackout is not easy, after all, though we have such a slick little phrase for it. I always think that a mother should be the one to do the telling. It was the last time we were together. She never came back from her next voyage, and nobody could find out exactly what had happened to the ship. Perhaps they were all in blackout when whatever end it was came to them. Oddly enough, my father's father was on the same voyage; I believe he had intended it to be his last. But by the time I knew about it a good many Terran years had gone by. I was looking forward with intense excitement to my own first voyage.

I suppose one of the things which one finds it hardest to take is that one must develop a stable personality and yet that inevitably it will be altered by the other forms of life with which one will be in communication, and that these bio-psychical alterations must be accepted. And can only be accepted by the stable. And that the achievement of stability alone, even after what the mother has done in the first year, takes half an old-fashioned lifetime.

For the nursery world, up to thirty or thirty-five, there is nowhere like Terra, lovely old Terra that we have nearly destroyed so often! and all its amiable fauna, within reach

8

of normal affection. Above all, for the woman child. I may be out of date, but I always feel that biology and, of course, communication are essentially women's work, and glory. Yes, I know there have been physicists like Yin Ih and molecular astronomers—I remember old Jane Rakadsalis myself, her wonderful black, ageless face opening into a great smile! But somehow the disciplines of life seem more congenial to most of us women.

It always seems to me curious that there are some things in exploration that we simply cannot think will happen, in spite of all our warnings and examples. A failure of communication? Or of imagination? Does communication wipe out imagination, which is, in a sense, solitary? My group is working just now with some quite young volunteers, and we may get results. The difficulty seems to be that in the nursery world we take ourselves for granted as stable personalities, as completely secure. Impossible that we should ever deviate, that interference should ever be a temptation. Not for us, we think. How young can one be! And this in spite of books, films, contacts of all kinds. It is of course simply that one has to be over-stable in order to stand up to later impacts, and the fact of this over-stability makes one unable to guard against what will certainly happen, as one might have guarded had one felt oneself in any way weak.

It all works out in the end. But the impact of other worlds on this apparently immovable stability comes as a surprise. Nobody enjoys their first personality changes. Most of us have at some time tried out some of the hallucinogens which do produce temporary change, but somehow that does not prepare one as much as is supposed. Not at least in my experience. Occasionally, even, in an attempt to rock personality, young people try the experiment of becoming temporary carnivores. I never did that myself, but then, I am greedy, very much aware of the taste and texture of what I eat. Besides, I think a communications girl would be bound to find it impossible;

there is no edible life in Terra which cannot evoke some slight empathy for any of us.

Although, of course, I longed in the normal human way for exploration, I found my first world oddly disconcerting. I remember it so well! Naturally they don't start one on completely unknown or very dangerous loci and luckily too there is an infinite—or is it infinite? Oh well, that's not for me to say—choice. I was thought to be good at communication (I am, of course, or you would not be understanding this page which you are reading) so I was teamed up with other experts, all youngish, except for our leader, Peder Pedersen, the mathematician. How lucky I was to start with him. How very lucky.

There is something fascinating about the detail of one's first space journey. They get terribly boring after a time, and perhaps that's as well or one would have less opportunity for contemplation which, after all, needs conditions of slight discomfort. Normally nowadays I contemplate during the whole of the space flight, whether in or out of time, but in those days I had not yet mastered any of the usual techniques of contemplation, nor would it have been normal at that age.

The world was lambda 771 in the Q series. Got there? Not an impossible atmosphere, and a comparatively minor gravitation problem. But communication had not been established. The difficulty was not in any kind of hostile attitude. That kind of thing has been almost entirely overcome, except in those few galaxies about which we all know. But in lambda 771 the inhabitants' evolutionary descent had been from a radial form, something like a five-armed starfish, itself developing out of a spiral. They were in several sizes from a few centimetres to almost a metre across. At first it was not clear whether these were young and adult forms or different races, but all of them had arms of a kind that could be partially retracted, flattened and so on, and which were studded with suckers which could be used to hold tools. Among their main art-

10

efacts were wide but low buildings, profusely decorated on the undersides of their roofs, mostly with spirally fungal and rooting forms. One had to go on hands and knees to see them, but it was well worth it. These creatures had a definite top and bottom, necessary after all for gravitation. But the radial pattern which had developed out of the budding spiral had remained throughout evolution and completely dominated all mental and psychic processes.

It is only in circumstances like this that we realise how much we ourselves are constructed bi-laterally on either-or principles. Fish rather than echinoderms. I knew this in a sense, but when it came to attempted communication it increased my difficulties far more than I ever thought it would. Also, I hurried over my acclimatising period, a silly thing to do, but young explorers are all the same.

I had to cut myself off entirely from the rest of the expedition, and I did not find it easy because I was by then strongly attracted to another member of it, T'o M'Kasi. He is still an outstandingly beautiful person, though he has, very rightly and properly, etherealised. He was not at all ethereal then; he had the delicious springy hair of his father's ethnic group, but he would never let me touch it—not at first, anyhow. He was a classical geologist then, though he has progressed since.

Well, I couldn't let that stand in my way, although I admit I allowed it to do so for a matter of hours. Then I got together my various transmission and reception instruments. I brought far too many, of course. One always does at first. I got to know more about it later. T'o came and watched; I remember he was trying to deal with some crystalline structures which he rather distrusted. With reason, as it turned out, but that wasn't until later. He was gloved, but he dusted his fingers together and took the glove off. His fingers were long and the colour of a well-cooked crisp biscuit; I seemed to feel them with my teeth and tongue. He said "You'll be careful, Mary? They may have a deliberate block against communication. If they

11

want to stop you, don't go on."

"So, how many expeditions have you been on?" I said, checking my circuits very carefully.

"Three," he said, and out of the corner of my eye I could see him coming nearer. And at the same time I did feel a little scared. Only a little, of course; I was passed as completely stable, and I was well aware that I would not have been taken on this expedition if it had been supposed that it was a dangerous assignment instead of merely tricky. "You'll remember the Jags?" he said, "never take your shieldings off—will you, Mary?"

"That's all right," I said.

He began to try and help me with circuits, but I asked him not to; it is a thing one has to do, after all, oneself. But I liked it that he had tried, and that it had brought his head so close to my hand that I only had to stretch my fingers—and there it was, the delightful heather spring of the different hair tension tingling against one's digital nerves as no flaccid blond hair does. He did not move his head away.

CHAPTER TWO

It was quite a problem to get through to those radial entities. Naturally I spent some time in the most unobtrusive
observing while I thought out the best communication
techniques to use. Their main organs were, of course, central and not orientated in any direction. I soon became
sure that any unevenness in the peripheral ring of brain-
plus-eye material was looked upon as a blemish, but one
was left in uncertainty as to whether this was supposed to
be moral or physical.

They also wore at times a kind of flimsy artificial covering which could either protect the ring or make it more obvious, and which appeared to be kept below the body, or
possibly to be exuded from the under part. It clung to
one's fingers if one touched it, and had a smell which was
entirely new to me and difficult to assess. It was extremely
hard to know what kind of thing this was without interference. And I was being very very careful about that,
all the more as it was my first world.

After a time, however, I realised that I must concentrate on what went on during periods of a rather strange
activity in which first of all one radiate would move under
a shelter and start to turn, first in one direction, then in
another; apparently the direction in which they began occurred entirely at random, or at any rate we never found
any evidence to the contrary. I am almost certain that this
was a kind of reversion towards spirality. In our world,
species which spiral do so in one direction only, but I do
not think this would have been the case with the ancestors

of my radiates. I found a small shell-producing form of life in this world, and was interested to see that its spiral went either way. At any rate, the dance would begin with one individual. Then another would become aware of this and approach. The two would lock together like cog-wheels, an "arm" into a hollow. Then, usually quite rapidly, others would appear so that in a matter of half an hour there would be a dense carpet of them, the inner ones locked together, the outer ones apparently in some agitation attempting to get inward, especially if there were so many that the shelter could not cover them. Had these creatures been descended from six-armed ancestors, the putting together would have been easier; as it was there were always gaps in the perfection of the carpet, even if the "arms" were retracted, expanded or otherwise adjusted. And it seemed as though the object was for all to come close and quiet and untroubled.

When this was achieved for a moment, the membranes covering the eyes, which were deep bluish green in contrast to the general brownish yellow of the body colour, shut down and the brain ring with its marked nodules at the central arm nerves appeared to flatten. We had some knowledge of the anatomy of these creatures owing to the fact that we occasionally saw one that had been killed by a type of insectoid enemy, not unlike mosquitoes, but up to thirty centimetres long, with extremely hard sucking jaws, which dropped on to the radiates from above. These were what we called jags. They appeared to be so nearly without consciousness of any kind that we were prepared to count them provisionally as not-life. Of course, one can communicate with all forms of life, however destructive and without consciousness; but that time has not come. Meanwhile it had enabled us on this world to do a dissection and preservation of one of the inhabitants. We could only hope that we had not interfered with any death or burial rites.

It was against these jags, we thought, that our radiates built their decorated shelters. Meanwhile, the jags dropped jaws first on to the eye ring, killing in a matter of minutes. None of them had actually attacked one of us, but there was always the possibility. Several times they had plummeted on to pieces of apparatus which had some glistening parts which might have appeared to them as eyes. We were taking no risks.

Once I had settled down with the radiates, I tried out various means of communication until at last I got my contact. It took me a long time, I remember. Nowadays I would probably have managed it all much quicker and with more certain jumps towards the solution of my problem, but after all this was my first world. There were days when I felt completely baffled, but I just could not go back and say to T'o M'Kasi, or indeed to any of the others, that I had been unable to get through.

I did meanwhile make a number of observations which supplemented those which other members of the expedition were making. I had decided that I had better, as far as possible, go around on hands and knees so as to be at the same aesthetic level as the rest of the inhabitants. Had I not done so, I would probably not have realised the nature of some of the movable artefacts. In fact, I could not always make out what, if anything, they were used for, but could admire them. I was looking at a rounded object in some material which I did not recognise, but which had decorations inside it, of much the same kind which from time to time in human aesthetic history workers in glass have been proud to produce. It was apparently something which was rolled round the eye ring by a muscular ripple. I could not see that it was in any way what one might call useful. And suddenly my aesthetic admiration appeared to meet an echo. I realised I had got through.

As usual in communication problems, the first step was

the most difficult. Once one saw what kind of rapport should be looked for, it was a matter of rapid assemblement of data. I had, after all, had the training. At one stage in my solution—or rather our joint solution, for the radiates were as eager from their side as I was from mine—I had a piece of luck. I saw one of the jags hurtling down and managed to kill it in flight. Oddly enough, I had never killed anything before. Terra, after all, is clear of enemies. I knew the jags counted as not-life, but all the same I was shocked at my own action. Not so the radiates.

Well, I won't bore you with my observations. The final findings of the expedition are all naturally in the Journal. I remember I made a most ludicrous mistake about their sex life! This was corrected in a later edition; it was all due to my own anthropomorphising. I had been warned about it often enough, but one never knows quite how these things will take one. Doubtless my subconscious drive was firmly fastened on myself and T'o.

However, my conscious concentration was all on the radiates. Gradually over a period of weeks I developed communication, first from generalised approval or disapproval and the simple harmonics to more complex and precise and mental aesthetic or mathematical statements. Then gradually we got on, once they themselves were cooperating completely, to further developments.

I had, of course, like a dancer to adapt myself to my communicators. That's the kind of reason why, as I've said, I believe communication science is so essentially womanly. It fits one's basic sex patterns. And the more I adapted to them, the more out of tune I became with my own normal concepts. Turning over on my mattress—I had one of those rather special ones then that fold into nothing and foam at a touch of any atmosphere; nowadays I meditate and don't need one—even that simple choice involving right or left seemed unnatural. Right hand or left—impossible alternations!

In communication, as, of course, you realise, by the constant succession of a or b, a or b choices, snap judgments and actions can be made as rapidly as possible in the semi-intuitive technique we have all learned, which is both mental and manual since it also involves instruments. I found these choice successions increasingly difficult to make. It was like walking in loose sand, a drag of other concepts.

One is so used to a two-sided brain, two eyes, two ears, and so on that one takes the whole thing and all that stems from it for granted. Incorrectly, but inevitably. My radiates had an entirely different outlook. As I got to know them better, I realised that in many ways they were highly—in our phrase—"civilised". But they never thought in terms of either—or. It began to seem to me very peculiar that I should do so myself, and that so many of my judgments were paired: good and evil, black or white, to be or not to be. Even while one admitted that moral and intellectual judgments were shifting and temporary, they had still seemed to exist. Above all, judgments of scientific precision. But after a certain amount of communication with the radiates all this smudged out. If alternative means, not one of two, but one, two, three or four out of five, then action is complicated and slowed to the kind of tempo and complexity which is appropriate to an organism with many hundreds of what were in evolutionary time fairly simple suckers and graspers, but which in development have adapted themselves for locomotion, food retention, tool-handling, the finer delicacies of touch and probably for other purposes of which I only became partly aware. It thus came about that with no sense of awkwardness, two or more choices could be made more or less conflicting though never opposite. Gradually I found myself getting into the same state of mind.

As I got to know my radiates as individuals—always a little difficult with a completely other species and one

17

tends to memorise individuality by inessential markings and deformations and such—the thing got more difficult. They did not name themselves as we Terrans do, and as we are apt to imagine most other worlds do. There were, however, group names shading into one another. Slowly I began to forget my own name.

It is obvious that their mathematics would be different, though I found it extremely hard to grasp at first. It seemed to be exactly what was needed for their technological purposes, and technology they had, once one became aware of what objects were natural and what altered in this particular world. The queer thing was that to my mind they were extraordinarily inefficient about the jags. Probably this was something to do with their sight; they did not, of course, focus through holes in rings of contracting muscles as we do. They perceived not two, but a great number of images of a much more diffuse kind, which built up into the sort of perception which one could guess at through their art. Naturally the vision was of the same quality all round, so that there was no front or back, but it appeared as though they were unable to see anything at a great distance above them—distance in which the jags flew and from which they plummeted. So the jags seemed to appear out of nowhere for no reason suddenly and inescapably. I felt if I could only get them to *try*! But that would have been interference.

They did make the decorated shelters, and so long as they stayed underneath them they were safe, but not when they went outside. Yet inside and outside was too sharp and opposite a distinction to be clear to them.

Nor after a while was it any longer clear to me. For I was coming more and more into tune with the five-choiced world. Naturally I did not realise it was affecting my own personality. I felt only that everything was going as it should be, was opening out, that I was appreciating more and more the thought and actions of my chosen world.

18

When their wheeling dances started, I found myself emotionally wheeling with them, even if in fact I stayed still, or almost still; I felt myself merging in an all-sided relationship, not merely eye to eye. On a further remove problems appeared to be solving themselves, though sometimes uncertainties remained which all the same did not seem to be relevant. It is not easy to recall all this, because thee actual words in which it is recalled are too sharp and unambiguous, plain uncompromising Terran words, often with exact opposites!

I also found that I was beginning to think of general philosophical problems in a way that seemed new and full of possibilities. And yet somehow I could not quite apply my mind directly to them in the way I had done in my Terran days. I would find myself in the evenings after work with an idea, or indeed with several ideas; these appeared to be graspable, to throw new lights on some kind of reality. Yet something, as it were, slipped. And then I found an equal slipping in my imaginations about T'o M'Kasi.

I had supposed myself to have made up my mind about him. But who was I? What my mind? I began to get the feeling that what was happening to me was on a par with what happens under the action of some of the hallucinogens, when the nature of perception is taken apart so that several aspects of the object normally seen as one are now seen separate. I remembered with some slight uneasiness that it took some time for the personality to re-integrate after some of these drug experiences, and I began to think I must go back to the rest of the Expedition. Go back? Back? It didn't have any meaning. Or did it?

Well, I got together my apparatus, my notes and my shelter with some fumblings, and then I got in touch with the others. I had sent messages from time to time to our base, as we all did while we were working on our own, but I had taken less and less interest in doing so and in what

19

they said in return. Any of them. Then something happened. I was wearing my shieldings but had lifted the eye mask; it was a pattern we had in those days which was apt to dim. I looked up and around slowly, I suppose in a way imitating the radiates, and was suddenly aware of a jag high up but coming straight at my eyes. And for a moment I was completely unable to save myself; the simple courses open to me: to snap down my eye piece, to duck my head so that the shieldings covered me, to raise my hand, to shut my eyes—all seemed so equivalent that I could do none of them. Luckily I reasserted my normal self, snapped out of it with a couple of seconds clearance, enough to duck forward so that the jag splintered itself messily on my shieldings. But I felt a good deal shaken. Looking down at the smashed-up jag, it appeared to me that my action had been random and unreasonable. Surely there should have been something else?

T'o M'Kasi came out to meet me. He seemed different. Or did he? Was it in him or in me, this difference? I couldn't even decide on what the difference was—if it existed. It was as though I was in some curious way elsewhere. As though he spoke to me from behind something. I couldn't place it. Then he said something that rang a bell. "You've been with them too long. You're thinking radially. Aren't you?" I supposed I was in a way, why shouldn't I? "Do you want to stay changed?" he asked. Changed, I thought, changed? We were under shelter now. I took off my shieldings slowly.

"We all got a bit like that," he said. "We found ourselves thinking like them. If we got in touch at all. And you've done it most, Mary. There's only one quick way to snap out."

"What is it?" I asked troubled. For now I felt very strongly that my personality had been shifted and that I didn't want it to stay that way. If I could be what I was—which meant being what he and I had been. "What is it? What do I do?"

20

"Make a choice, Mary. A quick two-way choice. But quick!"

"Give me a choice then," I said, and I still didn't know what he was going to say, although if I had been myself I would surely have known.

"Well," he said, "shall we have a baby?" I remember that I didn't answer. Couldn't. "Baby or not baby?" he said. "Two-way choice, Mary. Quick!"

Now I knew quite well what my original personality would have wanted and answered. I had made up my mind during my first week alone, while I was still studying the radiates, but was not yet changed by them, that it would be a good idea to have a baby on my return to Terra. It could even be conceived during the space journey, as this oddly enough had no ill-effect. It would mean taking two years off exploration, but I had several ideas about the theory of communication which I could work at. Some people, of course, preferred to make several explorations before they allowed themselves the pleasure of a baby, but I have always felt that this is rather a strict and even unbiological mode of behaviour. I had wanted also to have a pale brown baby. And I had wanted to touch T'o all over. I had wanted to get my fingers long and tinglingly into his hair, and to run them down his neck and arms. I knew that was what I had wanted; but I knew it as though I had been reading it in a book. And the book was in another galaxy. If only, I felt, the question had been asked then and T'o had looked at me as he was doing now—

I stood there in the base shelter among the Terran things, each with its definite use, which, somehow, made it peculiar and abnormal. With some interest I was observing myself at this moment not able to speak. It was impossible to do what one had once thought of as making up one's mind. It seemed ridiculous, almost wrong, to be faced with a direct positive or negation. I reacted against it. And yet I kept trying desperately, angrily, to find my

21

own personality and my own point of view, since it was to that surely that I would come back after this rocking and twisting? And quick, I said to myself, quick, and he under his breath was saying the same. But I couldn't get back to myself. I couldn't speak. I couldn't say yes.

CHAPTER THREE

Yes, that's the kind of jam one gets into. I got out of this one in time, but too late for T'o. Of course, it was all a long time ago, and I can only just remember my sense of being slewed off base, the astonishment and resentment I felt as I clawed my way back to normal. By the time I had got round to being again a two-choiced, definite personality who could say yes, T'o was away on another expedition. I didn't in fact have my first baby until some five years later. And altogether differently.

There had been two expeditions first—and naturally when I speak of years I am talking in terms of subjective years. Clock years have, after all, ceased to make sense, though we use them in childhood and adolescence. They must have been useful at some time, but that was when we were still at the mercy of clocks. When I came to talk this over with others in my age group, I found that their personalities very often took a knock on their first expedition, and then re-stabilised more firmly. That may well be the normal pattern for explorers. I don't think the Martians ever have quite the same difficulty, but it is rather hard to formulate the right question which will give one the information. I never managed to, even with Vly.

Oddly enough, it was my second expedition which nearly finished my career. This was to an Epsilon colonisation. You'll remember the Epsies; they were among our early contacts, after we first began Galaxy travelling, and in some ways an extremely helpful one. Though I believe it put some people right off space exploration. The Epsies were well ahead of us in their space theory, and also in some aspects of chemistry, and perfectly willing to share information, once we had got over the initial misunderstandings (which were extremely unpleasant for those concerned, though long before my time). Yet somehow I couldn't like the Epsies. As a child one learns to love all life, but inevitably some more than others. Being human, one cannot be neutral. And the Epsies were distressingly like centipedes; their mouth parts had developed along the same pattern, and they had the same flattening, due no doubt to the exigencies of their original world and the necessity of having to hide between the layers of the purplish shaly-looking rock which jagged up all over their home planet.

Of course they had long outgrown this need, though their dwellings were still in thin layers—not that this wasn't architecturally interesting, once they had their building materials completely in control—and their enemies had been extinct for a couple of millennia. But once evolution has gone so far in a certain direction, one cannot do much about it, as many forms have found to their cost. The patterns harden; mutations cannot change the structure. And anyhow the Epsies thought they were fine as they were, just as we ourselves do. The metal decoration which they tended to wear exaggerated the very features which the human observer was humanly bound to like least.

We humans—and it is almost the same for males as for females—like creatures which are warm, rounded and pleasant to the touch and smell, although smell, of course, is the most individual and subjective of the senses. If we find creatures of this kind we are prepared to give them sympathy, and to think of them as like ourselves, even if they are non-intelligent. But the Epsies had none of these lovable qualities; they were only intelligent. Their brain material spread along their rippling sides, and when answering difficult questions they stiffened in a typical and recognisable way. In intellectual repose their legs rippled even when they were not actually progressing, and in fact the upper third of their bodies was usually held upright. But they enjoyed being asked questions, and I sometimes thought that this was due to the definite *frisson* of momentary immobility which questioning gave them.

I was, of course, on communications; that was to be my speciality during all my earlier expeditions, and indeed I still find the old problems very pleasurable to work on. Communication technique had been reasonably well worked out by the first and second expeditions to the Epsie home world, but there were some loose ends to be picked up. I had looked forward to doing this, even after seeing 4D films of my future contacts. I felt that, although at the moment I could not see how, I was bound to learn to love them. It never happened.

The atmosphere and gravity no doubt made it more difficult. The gravity was not so bad as on many worlds, but it was certainly tiring, even with the usual booster technique, and bad for the feet; we all did foot exercises every day, but we had to be very careful about our individual atmospheres. This kind of thing becomes automatic, but I was faintly uneasy most of the time. I was with Peder Pedersen again; he had warned us against hallucinations; the slightest leak and they began. I remember once I thought I saw T'o.

The Epsies had colonised very vigorously, and at a period of moral crudity, which luckily humans had lived through and put behind them by the time they reached the technical excellence in space travel that the Epsies had achieved earlier. This new planet of theirs was, to our eyes at least, much pleasanter than the original Epsie world. The vegetation was beautiful, in shades of apparent blue, and exquisitely shaped. There were winding lakes of what could have been water. And there were local fauna with which one immediately felt sympathy.

It was not that they were genuinely hominid, but one felt as though they were. They had rounded heads, large dark eyes with eyelashes, paw-like hands, and a genuine playfulness. The Epsies didn't play; they asked and answered questions, decorated themselves, elaborated their dwellings and their technical organisation and were undisturbed by their infrequent matings. These produced enormous broods which soon became independent but had to be fed. The Epsies were carnivorous.

At one time only a certain percentage of these large broods survived. It was due to their increasingly high survival rate that the colonisations had become urgent. We had, of course, made a special study of this before the expedition. Our homework, we called it, for it was all done on Terra. It was clear from the 4D films that the Epsies' killing and eating habits were distasteful. Yet this was nothing very new. I remember Peder Pederson glancing at a picture and saying to me, with a grin: "You've got to think yourself behind that mouth." This was quite a difficult exercise, but of course necessary before communication could be properly established, and I was on my toes to do better than the last expedition. Thinking oneself into the shape of one's contact was elementary when considering communication techniques, but sometimes one had to be very careful to think oneself back.

The last expedition had intended to go to this planet, but had in fact spent all its time in the original Epsilon world, where there was so much information to be passed. Peder just hinted to me that membership of this last expedition had been, well, almost over non-biological. One doesn't want to criticise another discipline; but one knows what molecular chemists are like. And the Epsies had plenty for them. Their atmosphere produced some very peculiar complexes, which left our dull old carbons in the stone age. I can't find this very enjoyable myself, but to some people it's jam.

Well, it was the usual thing taking off. The gadgets, the excitement, the blotting out of time. And then this world, lovely, except as I said for the atmosphere and to some extent the gravity. I had already decided what type of communication block I must overcome, and was quite excited at the prospect. The Epsies had been warned of our coming, and had an area ready for us. They had even put up structures in which we could have our own atmosphere—rather ingenious really, with interpenetrating passages for their own atmosphere and ours, so that they could come into our house and communicate through a system of cleverly devised locks—if one could call them that. We all expressed our thanks and satisfaction, but the building material was transparent throughout, and I confess it gave me a very curious feeling to have the Epsies flatly slithering at the far side of a transparency. This was all the more marked since they had not been quite able to imagine the non-flatness of humans, and most of the rooms were a tight fit sideways. There were only one or two places where we could pass one another at all comfortably. It was specially awkward for Peder Pedersen, who by now had developed a certain Scandinavian type solidity. But the lack of basic privacy was unpleasant, and when that was complicated by the presence of very slight leakage at one or two of the communication locks—we soon found out which—with resultant hallucinations, most of us began to react badly.

Naturally one could retire to the old ship for a rest; when Peder Pedersen's language had relaxed completely into archaic Norwegian swearwords (curious that they remained theological rather than sexual for so long, I developed quite a theory about that) the rest of us always got him to go back. I remember asking one of them how old they thought he was. He seemed at the time quite immeasurably older. Odd that I should have thought that. But I didn't go back to the ship much myself; I felt I had to make the most of my time.

Silis Grasni, who was on the original Epsilon expedition, but whom I met for the first time after I came back—she was over in Mars for a conference and, I expect, for the wines, most of the months of preparation before we left—told me that the colonist Epsies were probably rather different from the originals. "It takes a different type to be a colonist. It's the same everywhere. Even us!" said Silis. "The old Epsies would have used a bit more tact, though it would have come to much the same thing. Still it was a different species they used in the home world." I noticed she frowned a bit. "Not so endearing, perhaps. Though I liked them." By that time I knew what she meant.

Well, one has to make allowances for the colonist mentality. We know enough about it from our own history, but it was the first time I had met it in real life, and I had n other Epsie social standards by which to judge those in this colonised planet. The chemists of the other expedition had been singularly uninterested in biological standards.

During the first period I had only communicated with the Epsies who came into our dwelling. We did disentangle some of our problems, and I was able to ask questions in different scientific and philosophical disciplines from those that had been used before. All this was interesting and satisfactory, but soon I began to ask myself what other biological entities might be contacted on this planet. Our botanist, who was enjoying himself in the blue groves, thought there were distinct possibilities. And that way I began to become aware of the round-headed, dark-eyed fauna.

My play approach met with an immediate response, and

I soon found that they made shelters, decorated them-selves with fringed, blue leaves, and a kind of shining nut-like growth, and plucked their sparse silky fur into pat-terns. And then I found that part of their play activity was something which I could only think of as singing and danc-ing. Indeed, so much in sympathy did I become that I found this beautiful and moving, to the extent that at first I suspected it might be partly hallucinatory until every test I could devise showed that it was not.

Their main characteristic I suppose was liveliness. It is not altogether easy to say what one means by that. As they moved quickly, slipping in and out of the blue groves, bouncing rhythmically over fallen vegetation, handling and tossing with their fingerlike, rapidly moving front or hind paws, above all dancing, they seemed to give off a brightness which might have had something to do with the circulation of a blood-like substance, about which later we were to find out far too much, under their semi-transparent skin and light fur. They quarrelled, slapping at one another, or displayed and chased in a pleasing sexual activity. As soon as I came into contact with them I was never tired of watching them and joining with them in so far as the clumsiness of my atmosphere suit and the gravity pressure allowed. They used to gaze at my eyes, and dab at them quickly with paws or lips, but the window kept them out. I felt how much I would enjoy a still closer contact.

Naturally I tried to communicate. I did not hide this, and I also began to question the Epsies. It became ap-parent that there was some close relationship between the Epsies and these others. At last I found one of the Epsies who obviously knew all about it. We always found it dif-ficult to tell them apart; that's always so, of course, with some species towards which one can have no emotional feelings. Perhaps if one had allowed oneself to hate the Epsies, one could have told them apart. But hate is something of which no explorer should ever be guilty.

Anyhow, this one was larger than the rest, and highly decorated; his feet were all inlaid with various metals which gave a very striking effect while they rippled. Our communication was, of course, not in sounds, and they were uninterested in proper names (assuming even that they had them). Among ourselves we called this one Glitterboy. He seemed to enjoy particularly being asked questions about the other fauna. They seemed to have a name for them allied to the concept of a sphere or circle; I translated it "The Rounds". It seemed to have something to do with their eyes and head shape. He let us know that if we wanted to find out more about the Rounds, we should come with him at a time he would indicate. Peder was much interested, and said he would come too. The rest were all involved with their own problems.

My next attempt was to communicate with the Rounds with regard to the Epsies. This was the more difficult, because I had no notion of how much aware they were of the other species. I started by showing them pictures, up to life-size, but they had no idea how to perceive or organise the information from pictures. Then I got one of the others to help me make some 3D flimsies, which, after a lot of frustration behaviour, they did finally recognise. The reaction then was one of anger. They beat at the flimsies and tore them and a few ran away. I began to wonder what I was likely to see.

"You have to remember the third rule," said Peder Pedersen.

"Non-interference," I answered automatically, for it is drummed into one so thoroughly. And then "But you don't think—?"

"You're getting to like the Rounds, Mary," he said. "And it's difficult to like our intelligent friends." He nodded towards the utterly separate but so very intimate passage within inches of our cheeks and hands. There was an Epsie at the far end, clearly, I thought, longing to be questioned. "It's simpler to be in a world," he went on, "where none of the body structures and none of the moulds of action or thought are sufficiently recognisable for us to take up moral attitudes about them." I remember that as I backed out—for of course the room was too narrow for anything else—I began to have considerable misgivings about what was going to happen. However, it was a few days before we got the indication from Glitterboy. Meanwhile I did a good deal of outside exploring. Besides the Rounds, there were various rather odd-shaped fauna, ranging from a jelly-like thing that oozed about among the blue groves, to a gregarious type rather like frogs on stilts, small flying forms, reddish crawlers which my Rounds used to pull up by their tails, although they did not eat them, and a large nocturnal animal which I never managed to see clearly. We experimented gingerly with the vegetation, eating very small quantities. But to us it was all completely inedible; that's one of the disappointments of a new world, at any rate for young explorers: so often one finds something which gives one the feeling that it must be a still more delicious plum or peach, but how rarely it is!

The time came. Glitterboy indicated that we should go with him. I was glad of old Peder plodding beside me in his atmosphere suit, feeling the gravity which gave him various kinds of aches and pains, which he never spoke about as such, but which were clearly what he often swore at. There was no conveyance on this planet; it was not something which the Epsies had put their minds to, possibly because so much sensation, and perhaps emotion, was located in their feet. I doubt if they became tired in any way which would mean anything to humans. Even I got rather tired, young as I was then. I remember Peder saying to me, "Mary, you'd better sit down and rest." I thought at the time that he'd said it to give himself an excuse, so I duly sat down with him beside me. But now I am sure he was really watching me, and really felt I was tired. He was used to his own aches.

But Glitterboy poured himself over rock and gravel, under the fronds of the waving blue trees or their fallen trunks. When moving, the front third of their body, which was erect during questioning, went back on to the ground and went into action. His feet made a scuttering rattling noise. What seemed odd to me was that there were no Rounds to be seen, though I noticed plenty of the jelly lumps and stilted frogs.

Before we left I had asked Peder if we should take weapons. All expeditions carry these for defensive use in utmost emergencies. And of course to destroy oneself or one's friends comparatively painlessly in certain eventualities—though only too often if these occur one has not got the weapon. I knew how in theory they were used, but absolutely not in practice. Peder smiled and said he would take what was needed. I had better not. "Remember, if you feel yourself in danger, ask questions," he said, "questions!"

We now came to one of their buildings, a sheer wall of some glassy substance, a chemical combination which the atmosphere made possible. Glitterboy began communicating, telling us that now we should see the use of the Rounds. Suddenly I noticed that his mouth parts were moving very unpleasantly—or unpleasantly to me. I remembered being told earlier on, when watching the film, to get behind that mouth. I couldn't do it now, but I tried to show nothing.

As always in the Epsie structures, the door was hinged at the top; Peder and I had to bend. We straightened ourselves in a high and narrow courtyard whose walls had a few very steep, very narrow staircases sloping up them, apparently to reach a parapet which ran along the top. And the courtyard was packed with Rounds, and they were in a really terrible state of agitation, fear and anxiety

32

and violence. Some were running and leaping, others seemed to have frozen into unnatural postures. Some sang, but not the songs which had gone with the dances or the sexual play. And I could see that Peder could not recognise it as singing, though I, having been with them more, certainly did. The whole thing began to remind me of something I could not place. And then I did. It was a set of photographs which I had seen during my social history course. These were of what used to be called inmates of a mental hospital, a "bin" as they said in those days, into which violently agitated people could be shovelled out of sight. What I saw had been a combination picture made up from these photographs, and it was exactly how the poor Rounds looked, except that they had this glow which I had noticed before, during periods of action, coming off them.

Glitterboy erected his front third and began to communicate so fast that I couldn't pick it up. Some seemed to be organic chemistry formulae, and from my subsequent interpretation I suppose this was about the blood, or blood-like liquor, which was circulating so rapidly and invitingly to him inside the Rounds; and also about the chemical needs of his own body, of which he was accurately aware. But there was something about the tone of the whole communication which was startlingly repulsive. Yes, and dangerous. Dangerous even to ourselves. I looked at Peder. Through the window of his suit he gave me a look which said *question*.

"What use—" I began, and again Glitterboy poured out more information than I could channel, and suddenly he made a rush at the Rounds. So did several other Epsies who had been quiescent close to the walls. A door hinged up at the far end, and the Rounds began pouring through in a panic that translated itself to me as *No, No, No*!

But Glitterboy had rippled up one of the staircases and on to the parapet. I thought we had better follow, since I did not at all like the idea of going through the gate with the Rounds. The stairs were difficult, too steep for the gravity, too narrow for something without a handrail on the drop side. It was worse for Peder, who positively bulged over the drop. Nor was the parapet at the top any too wide. But perhaps it was as well that our own slight peril did take our minds off what was happening below.

For Glitterboy now seemed to be holding some kind of metal instrument, as unfamiliar in shape as the rest of their tools. Then I saw what it was for. As the Rounds passed under the door with their heads down, he or another put this or a similar instrument over their heads and pressed it. As this was done, each of the Rounds gave a little thin high yelp, only just audible through the hearing locks in our atmosphere suits. But then they ran on. They ran through a still narrower passage and into another courtyard. And then they seemed to settle down.

Yes, that was definite. They were wandering about, not jumping or yelling or singing or expressing any violent emotion, and apparently in no pain. We walked carefully along the parapet until we were above them. I noticed then the peculiar shine or glow of activity had died out of them. What had happened?

I then noticed that a few of them were being herded, gently and without trouble, into a still further enclosure between high walls. Glitterboy scuttled rapidly in that direction, and dived down the wall. We looked at one another, and Peder shook his head slightly. We went on watching the Rounds. In so far as I could pick up what they were communicating, it was assent. Some of them had settled in sitting or lying positions. When one of the Epsies came up to them, they did not seem perturbed, though even the flimsies had thrown them into such rage and terror before.

But inside the further enclosure? Suddenly Glitterboy came slithering up out of it. There was something dreadful dripping from his mouth parts.

Silis told me afterwards that in their home world the Epsies did not drip. But Glitterboy was a colonist. He stiffened, raising his much inlaid feet in the pleasurable attitude of one being questioned. I asked him quickly what he had been doing, and he answered, as I had expected he would, in biochemical terms of absorption but with a certain excitement. He indicated that we should see—and perhaps even share in—the process. It was, of course, essential that, as members of an expedition, we should observe and, as far as possible, participate, but the Epsies had realised that their substances were inedible to Terrans. It was only an outburst of enthusiasm that had made Glitterboy offer us the treat.

We did, however, observe, take notes and question. It was as we had supposed. The Rounds in the enclosure were set upon and sucked by the Epsies. They seemed to contain from seven to eight litres of bloodlike liquor, more for their size and weight than humans. The dry bodies—for the sucking process was thorough—were processed and used as building material. They did not seem to object very much to what was happening, though most of them winced at the initial puncture. Certainly they were not afraid. When Peder communicated a question about the circulation of this blood-like liquor, Glitterboy and another Epsie obligingly ripped open the body of a living Round. The circulatory organ was unexpectedly high up, but then there was no lung structure comparable with that of mammals. The most familiar anatomical feature was the brain in the head, though under a skull that was membranous rather than bony. That made it easier for the Epsies to give it that little nick which turned the fighting rebellious Rounds into docile and unanxious entities, and which also slowed the circulation, thus making ingestion somewhat easier and less messy. If that mattered.

Even the Round whose internal structures were exposed for our interest did not seem to be in even minor agony or fear. Discomfort, yes. But that disappeared in dying. Leaving the agony with me.

Peder Pedersen and I pieced together the rest of the story. Not all the Round population was taken, but enough to last for some time. The rest, breeding, would fill their place. There had been a time when they had been corralled, but the brain had not been nicked. Then there had been scenes. I got the nasty feeling that Glitterboy at least regretted them. Now it was almost too easy and unquestioning. Yes, in the old days the Rounds had occasionally turned on their Epsie captors, jumped over them, scratched with their paws at vulnerable eyes and brain spots, and quite often escaped—not all, but some of them. That no longer happened. All thought that the lifted gate was a way out; they could see some way beyond it their companions moving peaceably about. It was so arranged that they did not see the metal instruments.

I began to feel so full of hate for the Epsies that I could barely communicate. They realised that there was some failure, but did not know what. Peder Pedersen knew, all the same. He said to me through our radio link, which I remember distorted voices so that his sounded several tones lower than in real life and slightly crackling, "Anything you think of doing means interference." I knew. I knew. And yet I could not bear it. I felt myself gasping. I knew that if I had been the one with the weapon I would have had my hand on it. "I have seen much worse," said Peder Pedersen, "without interfering."

I looked down at the Rounds and Epsies, and felt myself rocking slightly on the edge of the parapet, recovered, but with a jerk that strained my atmosphere suit. In the mild leak that followed I hallucinated an extraordinary series of religious episodes. Naturally one learns the whole strange history during one's adolescence, and often re-lives some earlier religious experience. I had as a girl been more attracted by some of the early twenty-first century developments of Islam. But these hallucinations were wholly Christian, including a crucifixion in which the protagonist was ripped up and bled and bled endlessly. I remember pointing out to someone or something that the heart was in the human position, but could easily and somehow be shifted to become the Roundian circulatory organ. All sorts of entities which I had seen in books and films came to lap up the flowing blood, and at last the Epsies.

As is so often the case in hallucinations, the whole thing appeared to take in a vast stretch of time, although on the clock of pulse and respiration rate it took only seconds. But I was aware in some corner of remembrance that the overt practice of Terran religion in another world counted as interference; it was a very old decision not of much interest now, since few expeditions included persons genuinely interested in such things. Yet it appeared to me that the only way to achieve my end was to mount the cross myself and to bleed, explaining in a loud voice that I had not been nicked, that I was fully aware, and that this blood was freely and for ever available instead of the blood of the Rounds. I struggled to communicate this to all the different worlds, at the same time commiserating with myself that I was irrevocably fastened to a piece of heavy wood and so could never any more be an explorer. But then I felt hands on me, Terran hands, and a voice saying "You must get down, down—" and the faint crackling of Peder's voice. Down—how could I get down off the cross? But somehow I had to. Then the hallucinations began to fade out, and I saw that Peder was tightening the strained joints of my atmosphere suit and was pushing me towards the steps—there was another set, equally steep, equally narrow, on the outer side of the wall.

I climbed down somehow with a post-hallucinatory headache beginning to bang at the base of my skull. Inside the walls it was still going on, the full horror. On the way back, Peder Pedersen began over the crackling link to tell me about his childhood in a still fairly remote part of Terra, of the snow melting and the birches beginning to leaf, of the berry-picking children and the midnight sun, of the northern lights which were so wonderful before one's eyes were set on the galaxies and far stranger sights, and will be wonderful again when one is old and decides to retire for ever to the kind breast of Terra. Somehow it took me back to my right mind. I rested for an hour or two in the ship, out of sight of the Epsies, till the headache and the hate had worn off.

Yet in a sense the hallucination held me. Could I have done anything, somehow, along those lines? I could not see how. I cannot yet see how. And yet even now I feel that I ought to be able to see. But at the time all that I felt was deep shame. I was utterly humiliated because I had been so helpless. Somehow I had failed, perhaps betrayed, those whom I thought of as my friends. This feeling went on during the whole duration of the expedition, nor had the fact that I managed to break through some of the communication barriers which had baffled my predecessors to the Epsie world helped to lift me up. It was only during the slowdown at the end of the flight, with thoughts of Terra imminent, that I talked about it to Peder Pedersen. I remember he said to me that humiliation, however it was produced, was a necessary stage in exploration. The confident and equable could never be the greatest explorers. It was difficult to understand at the time, though I think I understand now. He said that one must be ready to be taken in, even if that meant being laughed at afterwards, because there must be no barriers between oneself and other entities. Disbelief must always be suspended. Humiliation. Out of the very bottom, when the moral and intellectual self one so carefully builds up has been pulled down, when there is nothing between one and the uncaring trampling foot of reality, then one may at last and genuinely observe and know. And the process of humiliation, Peder said, must happen again and again.

That isn't how one used, as a young person, to imagine the great explorers. But I am inclined to think that there is something in it.

CHAPTER FOUR

At first the feeling of failure and humiliation was only painful. I could not face the preparation for another expedition, and yet I knew the moral problem of the Epsies and Rounds was a fairly simple one, which had, in fact, been met in some form by several expeditions. If only T'o had been there. He could have picked me out of my pain, and we could have been happy on Terra. But that didn't work out; our subjective years didn't seem to synchronise. I couldn't even write up my observations properly. Peder Pedersen was extraordinarily sympathetic, but busy on another expedition. He asked me to come, but I didn't. I couldn't.

I became mildly interested in certain aspects of immunology, and hung around with the immunologists at one of their centres. Then something turned up which flipped on the current. As you know, alien tissues call up antibodies from the living mammalian body. But take a tissue so alien that it is not recognised even as an enemy so that no anti-body is produced. And suppose again that it is also of a kind which can symbiose with a mammalian host and develop? This was for long purely a theoretical supposition. Then suddenly it became possible. The type of life in a small and isolated world had exactly these requirements, and some specimens had been brought back; everyone had agreed that they were too far from intelligence to make this morally questionable. The beings there regenerated entirely from quite small parts, much as we have all observed with the common earthworm. If kept in a suitable environment, they developed into the whole animal, but on a very small scale and barely viable, though it was possible to feed and cosset them into something like adulthood.

But if they were grafted on to a host, they not only survived but became of a normal size, almost a metre in length. After that a neck formed between them and their host and normally they detached themselves. They appeared at first sight to be somewhat shapeless, if anything faintly repulsive. One got the feeling that they were at the evolutionary stage where they might develop in one of many possible directions, but this was, as it were, undecided. The behaviour of the grafts made this idea seem more plausible. It would have been inaccurate to speak in terms of intelligence, but certainly there was an organisation of behaviour and sensibility which gave a definite character to these beings. It was entirely meaningful to talk of pleasure and pain, of memory, anxiety and possibly affection in relation to them. They had no bone structure, but a certain degree of what looked like cartilagenous stiffening. They were not unpleasant to touch, with an outer layer, normally fairly soft, which could be hardened, apparently at will. They could also, again apparently at will, extrude pseudopodia, usually three or five, which helped them to writhe along, and might well be useful for other undefined purposes. They could ingest food, though in laboratory conditions it had to be thoroughly macerated. They could perceive certain kinds of nearby objects, at any rate, though it was not certain how. Some types of object or stimulus seemed to induce activity; they could writhe and roll quite quickly towards or away from something they had perceived.

But what kind of perception was it? There appeared to be no differentiated organs; it was, in some way, an overall effect, quite unlike anything Terran, or indeed most extraterrestrial life. The whole thing was baffling, and I came on it first in my communications role. I was equally baffled, but most interested.

The grafts had been done in the first instance on various experimental animals, dogs, pigs, jackals, horses, the amiable Martian znydgi, and a few other species. The results had been unforeseen. Behaviour was, apparently, picked up to some extent at least from the host, for instance it was plain with the grafts on dogs. All the dogs in this centre liked the laboratory technicians, and one of them in particular who was the dogs' regular contact; so did the grafts, wriggling eagerly towards the preferred person. With the znydgis, who were without affection, though so amusing and peaceable, the grafts made no motion towards the technicians. But neither were they afraid. It also looked as though the jackal and hyaena grafts did better when their food was mixed with meat juices; the same diet when given to horse grafts was not acceptable.

One or two grafts had been made on wild animals which had deliberately been conditioned into dislike and distrust of some or all of the animal house technicians. This passed to the adult grafts, which shrank or hardened and retreated from the relevant people. Of course, it was all far more complicated than this, and while I was there a number of neo-pavlovian experiments were being made. There were also, of course, a great many anatomical and cytological observations, which would have to be followed up. This involved ethical questions; they had been originally brought from the parent world on the assumption that they were completely below any level of consciousness, far less intelligence, which would have made such an action even doubtful. The experiments on grafting were made by excising pseudopodia, which could apparently be done without in any way affecting the donor. But if there was any attempt to take a piece of the main body, whether or not the pseudopodia were extruded, it caused discomfort, perhaps pain, and a remembered aversion to whoever had done it or attempted to do it. But was this memory, again, an unlocated, all-over effect?

In fact, the whole thing was puzzling. Not much was known of their home world. It had not been thought to be particularly interesting or rewarding, and there was not likely to be an expedition there for some time. But that was no reason why research should not go on. The next stage obviously was to try out the graft technique on a human host.

I was talking this over with Pete Lorim, one of the immunologists; he said it wouldn't be too difficult; the graft would only take two or three months, and for the first month would cause little inconvenience. But his own difficulty was that he and Silis Grasni were seeing a great deal of one another—in fact it was through her that I had got to know the immunologist group in the first place. He thought that soon Silis would let him father a baby, and he wasn't at all sure how she would take it if he had a large graft attachment. Naturally one does not criticise another scientist in the middle of an experiment, but if he is to father one of one's children one may well be a little choosey. Silis was at that time very attractive—though I got rather tired of hearing people talking about her—and I saw he had a case. "You'd do it otherwise?" I asked.

"Of course," he said. "But I expect one of the others will. It's just a case of setting aside a couple of months—and being bored, I think."

And then I said: "I don't believe this is a man's job. You ought to get a woman to do it. She'd get a better relation with the graft."

He thought for a moment, then said: "It's not possible she might get too good a relation?"

"I doubt if that would be possible," I said. "After all, a really close relation might mean a possibility of communication—some kind of communication anyhow." And then I said: "What about me?"

Well, we settled it. I would come and stay at the immunisation centre. They had an exceptionally good book and film library; I could fill in a lot of gaps. I had another reason, perhaps not very high-grade. Immediately below the Centre there was a large area of vegetables and fruit, where a number of new techniques had been and were being employed. Some of the vegetables were straight Galactic imports, always carefully supervised in case they suddenly became too successful (you will remember the early Venus-weed which looked like solving everyone's protein troubles till it started blocking the Gulf of Mexico.) Some of the Health Administration crowd were pleasant enough and we had some interesting discussions. Naturally there were a good many of the Martian canal-irrigation vegetables. One can hardly bear to think of how short a gustatory range Terran vegetables and fruit have, even if one includes those of all zones, in fact one can almost understand how our ancestors were such determined carnivores.

I think, all the same, the texture of some of the Galactic vegetation, with the different carbon build-up, makes part of the difference. How lucky that our enzymes manage to lock on! There had been some very satisfactory graft-hybridisation, partly done by Silis. There were improved mangoes and an improved pear, tiny, but how delicious! One notes the tendency nowadays to have both fruit and vegetables smaller, so as to give more scope for kitchen harmonics.

However, greedy as I am, it wasn't my main reason. And, after all, one has these gaps of dreadfully utilitarian space-diet. But it certainly made the prospect of a long stay at the Centre much more tolerable. Meanwhile I observed the grafts in process, as well as the adults, as carefully and intently as I could. I very much wondered about the effect on the experimental animals who were the hosts. There was, of course, plenty of everyday communication between them and the laboratory technicians. A great deal had to be explained to the animals, or they might be acutely uncomfortable, and might—especially the carnivores—have had to be restrained in some non-ethical way. All of them had found the experience wearying, and were slightly out of health at the end in spite of extra feeding, and especially extra fluid intake, but all recovered rapidly once a graft was away, and it became easily detachable as soon as it was adult and had begun to move in its own way. Of course, the experiment was put into their terms, and for most of the animals it was something they did for their dearest humans out of their affection and loyalty, and so as to receive praise and more affection. The more active animals felt themselves much slowed down, and I wondered whether this did not go beyond what one would expect from the mere weight and awkwardness of the grafts.

One interesting thing was that both dogs and horses recognised their grafts days and even weeks later, apparently by smell, and it looked as though the grafts recognised them. This recognition pattern was less strong with the pigs, and absent for the znydgis. One big Labrador bitch still worried about her graft after several months, feeling that it should have changed or grown up, become more doglike in fact. Her own laboratory technician and I both tried to communicate reassurance, but not entirely successfully. She knew it was not a puppy, but a graft, and yet in a way she couldn't be sure. It was the same for the hyaena.

I got it across to the dogs that I was going to be like them and take a graft; some of them became concerned and agitated. But I could not find out whether they had disliked the process because of its physical discomfort, or for any other reason. At any rate there was no more I could discover, and what I was going to do fitted into my mood of humiliation; I would put myself into intimate relation with an unintelligent form of life. Could one go lower? Yet at the same time I was aware that it was also an exciting and novel piece of research.

We decided to put the graft on to my thigh, where there would be an ample blood supply. We arranged a kind of sling, so that it would not incommode me at all for the first weeks. None of us could be sure how fast it would grow, and indeed for a few days we were quite anxious as to whether it would take. It seemed almost as though after all anti-bodies were forming, but luckily that was not so; had it been, a completely new theory would have been necessary, and during the few hours when it had seemed possible, we were all talking about it in great excitement, but without any but the craziest notions of what it might be.

None of the earlier experiments had been done upon any of the primates; it always proved difficult to explain to any of the higher apes about any at all lengthy experiments which might make them uncomfortable. They co-operated willingly over everything with aesthetic interest, or that was in any way active or stimulating, and were, of course, on such friendly terms that nobody would have dreamt of coercing them. We did not know what effect grafts might have on the normal female sexual cycle. This graft was done at my suggestion in mid-cycle, and to our interest ovulation did not take place. As the graft grew, I began to have feelings of malaise, of the kind which one understands used to be common during pregnancy, though they are so no longer.

As soon as it was plain that the graft had taken, we measured it every two days. At first I was completely objective about this, but gradually I began to fuss in a way that was not at all normal to me, and that clearly surprised my scientific colleagues. I began to be possessive about my graft; I could not think about it coldly. If the sling containing it happened to bump into something, I couldn't rest until I had reassured myself that it was perfectly all right, as indeed it always was.

And then after about seven weeks, during which it had grown vigorously, it began to show signs of independent movement. By now my own activities were much curtailed, though I still could make my way slowly to the library. This had a sun room full of interesting and beautiful plants, some experimental, and here I used to lie with my graft unwrapped from its sling and beginning to move. My colleagues were always in and out, very often bringing me the extra food and drink—I had dozens of their improved mangoes!—which I found I needed. I used to drink twice as much as usual, and yet was unsatisfied. I felt how much I would like to swim, but even an ordinary bath was difficult with the graft. Sometimes I would sit with my hands and feet in water, but that, though soothing for a while, seemed to be not quite what I wanted. Silis came and talked to me about Pete, and Pete about Silis. And gradually, although I felt less well and unhappily less able to make use of the library, I came to terms with my feelings of humiliation.

I found myself thinking endlessly about the graft, or rather not thinking, but maundering about it. I could not think about it without a name, and I named it to myself with splendid inappropriateness, Ariel. I had a feeling it was part of me, in the same way that Ariel and Caliban are part of Prospero, as they are normally shown in productions of the Tempest—one of the plays which stand up best to really modern treatment with all the effects, and I happened to have seen it lately.

By the time Ariel had been two months grafted, it was displaying a considerable degree of life; it was very flexible, not having grown any stiffening, and started putting out pseudopodia. Soon it managed to turn so that it was nearer me, gradually beginning to overlap me, moving against my thigh, the pseudopodia feeling towards the central line of my body. At the same time I noticed my breasts were beginning to swell slightly, and the aureolus to darken.

Pete thought there might have been something of the same effect on the bitches, though it never led to actual lactation, but he was also definite that my graft was more active than the others. We discussed what behaviour patterns or choices might be best picked up from me. I thought that listening to some kinds of music might be interesting. Music no doubt goes in at the ear, but that is not the end. Beethoven, deaf, heard his music as he wrote it. So, two centuries later, did the strange genius Battacharya Three. We also decided that I should concentrate on some number theory. I thought I had better look at pictures as well, so tried taking in, on as deep a level as possible, both figurative and non-figurative art of various schools in the past and present.

I did all this with increasing intentness during the last two months. In fact, I kept Ariel for nearly four months. It had arrived at an apparent adult size and activity towards the end of the third month, and Pete was quite ready to do the separation. But somehow it was—how can I express it?—flesh of my flesh. I'd half expected at the beginning that one would feel for the graft as for a tumour, and be merely glad and relieved to be rid of it. But this did not happen at all. By now Ariel was more than three feet long. It liked to be as close as possible over the median line reaching now to my mouth and inserting a pseudopodium delicately between my lips and elsewhere. I discussed this activity with Silis, as its effect on me was somewhat disconcerting. She, I am glad to say, laughed and said I shouldn't worry. I can still remember, past any memory of my later children's fathers, the peculiar feel and taste on my tongue of Ariel's pseudopodium, something altogether of itself.

I still had this curious longing to swim. Perhaps in a different environment I might have tried it. But I felt silly. It reminded me, though, of some of my communications with the laboratory animals, who all got across the need for water. I talked more to the Labrador bitch, a beautiful, golden, warm-eyed creature, and one of the jackals, who had an equally good memory and ability to communicate. Both had wanted to wallow in water, but the bath furnished was too shallow. I felt that this would have to be followed up.

However, the link between the graft and myself was becoming narrower, barely more than a short stalk between us constricting every day, and increasingly being pulled at by Ariel's wriggling. One morning even that was gone; all that was left was a small area of roughness on my thigh which soon disappeared. Yet for an hour or so I could not bring myself to tell Pete. Instead of being relieved by the separation, I felt I couldn't bear it. I even cried a little. Then Silis came in; she helped me to my feet—I hadn't been able to do any walking for the last fortnight or so, and I felt weak. I had been lying on a wide low couch where everything was in reach. I looked down now on Ariel, who moved doubtfully and put out five pseudopodia and then settled on a part of the couch where I had been myself. Pete came in, and one or two of the others in his group, and said they would watch. A little exercise would do me good. But somehow I hadn't the heart to go far; I still felt weepy. My breasts ached, but lactation did not actually take place. When I got back poor Ariel was obviously agitated and anxious. I knelt, and immediately it wriggled and rolled up to me again.

It was a painful two or three days; I couldn't help feeling a certain degree of guilt, though this was most unreasonable, as everybody pointed out. But I spent a good deal of time with Ariel. The musical education was a tremendous success. If I was not there and Ariel was agitated, someone had only to switch on the music which I had taken in; it had an immediate calming and apparently pleasurable effect. How? These creatures, both as grafts and on their own world, had no specific auditory organs. This was an even stranger case of all-over perception. Nor did music seem to affect dog or pig grafts, though we thought it had some effect on one or two of the equine and bovine ones.

Yet pictures, however closely shown, were without effect. I wondered whether possibly the music arrived as direct vibration (I had noticed earlier that they usually seemed aware of vibration from machinery, centrifuges and so on, even when they were some way off), but musical appreciation, as it were, had come through me. One thing I noticed was that in the macerated food Ariel shared my tastes. There had to be plenty of fruit—mangoes for choice!

I kept on puzzling about communication, trying out various techniques, with no results at all. One thing was clear. Ariel and I always recognised one another even among a number of our own species. I could not say how I recognised Ariel, but I always did. One day I was worrying at this. I was on the floor beside Ariel, who had grown rather larger and had now developed a certain amount of stiffening. We were in my old haunt, the sun room of the library; when I smell certain flowers it still recalls the whole thing vividly to me. Ariel began to extrude a pseudopod, covering my hand which happened to be palm up. After a moment or two I realised that this was putting pressure on to my skin, now hard, now soft, and a few seconds later I began to ask myself if this was not following a rhythm—if so, what? Carefully, very carefully, I began to take notes with my other hand. And it was —a communication of pure number progression.

It was tremendous! I called in the others. We repeated our rhythms. I gave back pressures. It was slow, because it could only be dot-dash, but it was wonderful, it was a beginning. What possibilities there must be! If this was organised behaviour, it went far beyond anything we had ever got from terrestrial mammals other than ourselves.

But was it? Or did it come of Ariel and me being irrevocably part of one entity?

Well, that was a week of conferences that I shall never forget. As soon as the news broke they all came rushing over. It went far beyond the immunologists. We began to discuss on all levels. We had plans for mass grafting on to human and Martian volunteers. Then for a recolonisation of Ariel's world from educated entities. But—would that be interference? Philosophical and neotheological arguments exploded all round us. I began to feel very junior and a bit uncertain. And then—then Ariel died.

There was no warning. Nothing appeared to have gone wrong. Nor did we know of any normal limits to the life span of these entities. But one day I found that Ariel was completely motionless. I called Pete. We watched. A dreadful smoothness came over Ariel's surface. Then, under our eyes, Ariel dissolved, deliquesced, became undifferentiated material. Ariel, flesh of my flesh.

We did not know the answer. Could it be that Ariel had absorbed so much that there could be no existence apart from me? Yet there had been every appearance of a separate life and a lively one. It was not even as if the neck of the graft had been broken, as it usually was with, for example, canine grafts. The biochemical tests of the material which had been Ariel were unsatisfactory. But it appeared that I myself was completely unchanged. I had almost hoped I would not be. That was the measure of my grief.

For a time the conference buffeted me about on a sea of discussion, excitement, disappointment, uncertainties and plans. They talked about other human hosts, and further experiments; there would be plenty of volunteers. Oh yes! But all the time I felt I must tell them not to risk it, not to allow this unhappiness and loss to happen again. Yet I couldn't say it. I felt numb. And then I heard about an expedition which I thought would be interesting. The personnel were part Terran and part Martian, and that in itself was something that I had always looked forward to. It was likely to have some elements of danger and stress as well. And I looked forward to that too.

Silis and Pete helped me to make my preparations.

CHAPTER FIVE

There was more danger on this expedition than I had expected; much more. It turned out to be the disastrous expedition to Jones 97, as everyone called it. You will remember about that. I was one of the lucky ones. As a matter of fact, I can remember very little: it all becomes dreamlike in my recollection. I have only a vague feeling of the dark Jonesian landscape shimmering and crumbling. The blast which deafened me for some days does not exist in my memory. I can only begin to recollect clearly when Vly was in contact with me, communicating reassurance and affection with all that was in him. He was the Martian communications expert, my opposite number on this expedition. As you know, of course, Martians rarely speak, and only indeed in what they consider embarrassing situations. They communicate through the highly educated tactile senses. This started in their subterranean days, in the original darkness in which they lived for so many millennia; they have gradually learnt to communicate at a distance, their long-distance sight improving at the same time, but tactile communication is the quick and natural thing.

Dear Vly was communicating all over with his tongue, fingers, toes, and sexual organs. I felt so grateful; it was so kind, so kind of him. More especially when one realises that on a mixed expedition the Martians never wish to communicate with the humans except for strictly technical and scientific purposes. It was with this feeling of gratitude towards him, of tensions easing, that I came to waveringly. Or was it only gratitude? Might it have been something more physiological, less ethereal? Difficult to ascertain.

I could barely breathe; every heartbeat was a triumph. When I could at last focus my eyes and keep them on a given object, I felt an extraordinary well-being, not in the least contradicted by the pain I was beginning to feel where almost every muscle had been strained, and two or three bones broken. I was deafened too, and could not have communicated with my fellow human beings. In fact, as you will remember, most of the Terrans on the Jones expedition were killed; it was the Martian members of the expedition who rescued those who survived. Their tough and spongy shells were better adapted to what happened than the human covering of skin and muscle over brittle bone, and all their tactile areas were very well shielded; we humans had thought this world was sufficiently understood for safety, and had not taken sufficient precautions. How mistaken we were! One doesn't expect to lose four-fifths of the personnel of an expedition, and this included Von Braun.

I simply didn't take it in at first. Nor did Olga, whom I was to get to know so well later. It was her first expedition, and as a botanist she had been disappointed; the lichenoids on Jones 97 were dull, and certainly not beautiful; they appeared to have no biological or chemical properties of any interest. She had started looking for microscopic growths, and it was because she had been lying on her face peering into a cranny that she was saved. The Martians picked her up unconscious, as they did me, and lugged her back to the ship.

The Martians, of course, took off their protective coverings in order to communicate. This was always a tiny bit disconcerting, since in some ways they were so like ourselves, but their uncovered areas were slightly different. I remember Olga blushing a bright northern pink the first time she saw two Martians in full communication. "But," she said, "what are they *doing?*"

"Communicating—talking," I said. "yes, certainly, with their sexual organs. And remember they are all two-sexed; they only take on mono-sexual characteristics at certain specific times, and very seriously, Olga, my girl."

"It should be serious!" said Olga, and gasped a little.

"Yes, yes, of course," I said, though I didn't think so, at least not in that way, but after all it was her first expedition. And then I went on to explain how the uncovered and mobile sexual organs, which Olga had barely brought herself to look at, were not unnaturally particularly sensitive, and could communicate fine shades of meaning. I myself communicated through these organs for the finer shades; no, I had no sense of revulsion; that would be most unethical. "They found us terribly shocking at first, you know," I said to Olga, "the way we covered up what should be uncovered. They couldn't get used to it. They thought we must have some kind of horrible taboo against communication. As soon as we got properly into friendly relations with one another, which happened fairly early on, long before we started galaxy-trotting, they began preaching at us about it. The earlier explorers had their trousers pulled off, and were asked very sympathetically if they weren't happier that way."

I remember Olga threw her head back and laughed as whole-heartedly as she had blushed before. "Do they still think us horrible?" she asked.

I said I thought so, but they got used to us. Used to our funny habits and coverings, the curious monosexuality of our lives and the fact that we were all a little bit too big. Most of the Martians stood about four feet or a little more, and they never grew very heavy. They certainly didn't find us attractive. The mere fact that we looked something like them, but were really alien, was against us.

57

The instinctive repulsion could only be overcome by a deliberate act of empathy, only possible to the most intelligent.

It had been quite hard for the Martians to get heavy, lumpish Olga and me and poor Zeke, who died later on, back into the ship. Some of them were hurt as well, but that had not stopped them from trying to rescue any of us they could get at; some had been blown to bits. Vly was the only one of the Martians whom I could reasonably say was a friend. I knew the others quite well, but not in depth in the way I had got to know Vly. As they speak so rarely in words, and at ordinary times feel that it is wrong to do so I felt very much flattered and honoured when Vly told me his name in audible speech. (I could just as well say "hers" rather than "his" but for reasons which will be apparent it seems more appropriate to say "his" all through.) Apart from being a communications expert, he was a brilliant mathematician, and also a wine grower. Not that the long striped pods are anything like grapes, but the result is deliciously similar! So when he named himself and, with an effort, called me Mary, I felt that a barrier had been overcome.

So when I began to become fully conscious in the ship—we had taken off by this time—I was glad to have Vly there communicating. I wanted him all the time at first. If he left me to deal with navigation problems (various things on the ship were broken, and take-off had been very difficult) I became unhappy and restless. If I slept I would wake up whimpering for him. After a time I noticed that I was half undressed; the atmosphere suit had been cut away from my broken arm, the broken bone in my foot, and from the whole of my body which was coming up in bruises. It hurt me a little when Vly communicated, lightweight though he was, but I would sooner have had him there than nobody. I was not fully myself, and needed contact. I am sure it would have helped Olga if something of the same kind could have been done with her, but she had only practised communication with them on the botanical level. Nor would she have liked to be undressed. The Martians, of course, found it best to try to get into contact with those areas in the human body which had most tactile sensations. Normally they respected our taboos, but not in an emergency such as this.

Earlier on, before the disaster, I was the only one who was completely at ease in communication, though there was a certain general pick-up between human and Martian in more general terms and in mathematical symbols, which came across easily, at any rate between mathematicians on either side. Von Braun himself was always rather bad at it. Some of the Martians obviously disliked communicating even with me. But with Vly, the fact that normally Martians find Terrans rather repulsive was overlaid by pure scientific curiosity and the delicate empathy towards a fellow worker which I mentioned earlier. Gradually, as the days went by, I began to be able to breathe and hear and move again, though with some pain and difficulty. I began to realise what had happened: the destruction of my friends and fellow workers and the loss of our data. But it was in an atmosphere of reassurance by the Martians. They were as shocked and unhappy as the rest of us about the disaster to the expedition, and as anxious to learn from it as we were, but the actual death of the Terrans did not have the same emotional impact. Olga recovered rather sooner than I did. She was with Zeke when he died of his multiple injuries, but the Martians at least managed to communicate some confidence and reassurance to him, which she thought made it easier. We put his body in the deep freeze; there might be something to learn from it. Neither of us was a physiologist. And we all knew the horrid tendency of any large object pushed out through the locks to go into orbit.

Whenever Olga made her way over to me, slowly because of a badly bruised back, she always covered me up. I said, "Don't worry. They want as large a tactile area as possible for communication."

"I wouldn't like it myself," she said.

"Yes, but you're not a communications girl," I said. "I can't let anything stand in the way, and when we are doing accurate communications questions and answers, it's necessary to meet them half way."

"You're trying to make out what happened when everything smashed up on Jones 97, aren't you? That's what all the communication is about?" Olga said, and then she asked, "Is Vly male or female or both just now?"

I remember I answered, "Must be both. Unless the shock of all this brought on mono-sexual characteristics, but I haven't noticed." It did occur to me that this might be a possibility. I knew from Martian history that a really bad shock was liable to send a whole group over into one sex or the other for quite long periods, though they always recovered.

However, this went out of my mind during our slow and methodical reconstitution of what had happened on Jones 97. We had decided against a "natural" catastrophe, but we were uncertain what had induced it: whether what had happened was within the powers of the fauna which we had observed and tried to communicate with, or whether we had just failed to realise the existence of some completely other life form, possibly not in that actual world, but probably in the same system. Gradually the Martians and ourselves came to the conclusion that the answer must be somewhere along these lines, and only to be solved by further expeditions. We turned over possibilities of this, looking for and finding precedents, while emotionally the Martians and Olga and I felt ourselves in a warming solar loyalty together.

This looked like being a long voyage, as some of the ship's essential equipment had been destroyed, and we could not go into complete time blackout. We could slow down our basic metabolism so that there would be no trouble about food, atmosphere and so on, and so that time was partially dealt with, but we were certainly expending some energy and time in calculations and plans. After the first wonderful elation of returning life, I began to feel less well, and was uncertain of what the cause could be. Shock, I supposed. I asked Vly if all the Martians had found themselves equally in shock. He said that it was so, and added that most of the group discovered within a day or two that they had been sent into a condition of active mono-sexuality. "Look," he said. (I translate as nearly as I can into Terran.) By that time I was able to think so completely in Martian images and feelings that our communication was easy and always affectionate. Most of this was being done face to face and with finger tips. I did look, and when he pointed it out it was clear that even in their strictly practical protective suits, there was a certain differentiation. Yes, one could even see it in their faces, although their actual sexual organs showed little change, which was not unexpected considering how much they were used as areas not of sexual activity, but of communication. "And you, Vly, what are you? No, let me guess. You're a male."

That was so, he said, and then added that he hoped he had not inadvertently activated any of my eggs during the first phase of communication. "You were barely conscious," he said. "And I had to get as near as possible."

I was intensely interested. That, I am glad to say, was my first reaction. "Are you sure that can happen?" I asked.

"It is rare," he said. "But it has happened both as between the two major species and between znydgi and one of your animals, coatis, I think. But the results have, I believe, been haploid."

"I don't see why—" I said.

61

"Nor do I," he answered. "But I am no geneticist. Do you think it can have happened, and, if so, would it cause you inconvenience?"

Martian faces are not very good at expressing concern, but he actually vocalised my name "Mary, Mary" with an attention in it which was—well, perhaps what all intellectual colleagues should feel for one another, but seldom do. I said nothing for a minute or two. But some observations on myself which had puzzled me began to fall into place. I began now to be rather alarmed at the personal aspect of this, and that got through to Vly who reacted quickly with the assurance that it would be all right. I saw this less clearly myself. Naturally in Terran conditions, should an unwanted fertilisation (or, as in this case, activation) take place, which does happen occasionally, though rarely, it can be easily dealt with. But not in a space ship.

I thought very quickly about a number of aspects of what was happening. If this activation resulted in a living haplaid, what would it be like? Probably small, female, infertile. The brain? The body? What right had I to create this entity? I knew it could never be normal, but could it be happy? Could it love? Could it be loved? By me? No doubt the thing could be stopped, not in the usual way with complete safety and certainty, but somehow. Yet would not this be interrupting an interesting and perhaps valuable experiment? A haploid. The activation resulting in an offspring with none of the so-called father's genes, but the mother's doubled, so that recessives may come out of their dark somatic or psychic corners, and play havoc. Ought I to allow this? No, surely it should be stopped, now, now! I began to think of ways and means, and yet—

Then suddenly I thought how upset Olga would be, and that luckily seemed sufficiently funny to distract me. I felt the communication pressure of Vly's fingertips, but for a moment I was not channelling. This disturbed him very much. He hunted with his tongue, but I began to laugh, very rudely by Martian standards. Very worried, poor Vly searched for another good tactile area, uncovered my breast and began on it with tongue and fingers. This was so Terran—and yet, deeply, so un-Terran—that it took me a little while to restart serious communication. By then he had begun to suppose that he had done something, though he could not quite see how or why, which would completely block communication, and was himself so agitated that it came through badly from his side. Finally I got it that he was trying to say that if this had happened could I dispose of the activated egg? He was a bit muddled about Terran physiology, but then it was not his subject.

"No," I said, "I shall let it develop. It will be interesting." For I had begun to think that a space voyage of this length without time blackout would be tedious. Before I knew where I was, I was beginning to feel elated. I wanted to pass this on as quickly as possible. I reached for his sexual organ and began to communicate on that. It seemed most peculiar that in its non-communication aspect it should have any effect on a Terran.

How right I was about Olga's attitude! She was genuinely and dreadfully disturbed and grieved. It was only after I had put it to her that the voyage might last for apparent years, even with what time slow-down we could manage, that the thought of a new being began to appear attractive. But she asked me anxiously which Martians were male and which female, and rather stupidly avoided the males for some time. It was little use explaining to her that such a thing could only be the result of a very rare accident. No Martian male would ever conceivably want to fertilise a Terran female. The fact that Vly and I were genuinely fond of one another was something most unusual; our common work and knowledge had led to an empathy and absence of revulsion and awkwardness on both sides which seemed only possible between professional communicators.

It might have been possible for me to slow down my metabolism so that the development of the embryo would also be slowed down. In fact, with the complete time blackout in perfect working order this can be done. Silis managed it perfectly on one of her expeditions. Sometimes I wonder how old Silis would be if one counted her up in clock years. But of course one never does.

Anyhow, it couldn't be done this time for me. The birth was not too difficult, though it took place without some of the usual Terran safeguards. But naturally I had a theoretical knowledge of muscle relaxation, and, being a haploid, Viola was considerably smaller than a normal child, though very well-proportioned. She was, of course, entirely Terran, but I called her Viola to be as near as possible to Vly, who was finding himself very much involved. Martians have, of course, strong parental feelings, though the resultant actions sometimes seem odd to us. I told him that the Viola was not only a lovely, delicate and many-coloured flower, and a musical instrument, but also as near a two-sexed person as we get on earth. However, when I tried to tell him the story of Twelfth Night, it all became quite incomprehensible and possibly to him more than a little indecent.

I didn't really care; I was enchanted with my little creature, and so quite soon was Olga. Feeding was a slight problem, as her mouth was small for my nipple at first, but we accommodated. The voyage went on and on. We had almost all come back to our normal consciousness and metabolism for the birth and soon after, but one could not go on like that. We discussed it, Vly and I in particular. We were uncertain how the metabolism slowing technique would work on Viola, and already we both felt very responsible towards this tiny live thing, but in the end we decided we must try it; otherwise I at least would have had to keep a normal metabolic rate to match hers, and that would have meant a food problem apart from any other effect.

It worked out. We **all** slowed down. But this had never to our knowledge before been done in a young child, and it

64

clearly worked unevenly with her. As we approached our own galaxy, and began to allow time again, and as the solar system grew near and time quickened, as we began at last to get in touch with base, it was apparent that Viola had partly grown up; she developed so rapidly from babyhood to childhood that it seemed as though some arrested process was catching up.

I found it extraordinarily exciting. Certainly I got little of the instinctive slow-motion animal pleasure that one gets from the protracted babyhood of a normal human child, which I had with my later children. But I found this rapid and lovely unfolding something strangely light and joyful, most of all when it became clear that the small brain volume appeared to be making no difference to the I.Q. Every now and then I caught myself thinking that had this original accident happened on Terra, or indeed in the solar system, I would have ended the activation without even thinking of it as a problem, and how sad that would have been. This happy and delightful small entity, not entirely human, and yet mine—I remember so well the stab of tenderness towards her! And strangely, oddly, the same tenderness towards Vly.

CHAPTER SIX

I went next on a comparatively short trip, though it involved a communication problem which I did not manage to solve at all completely. There are plenty of them still. It was one of these global intelligences, not differentiated into somatic entities, though with some rather odd parasites; we had originally decided to communicate with them, and there had been trouble. Of course, this wasn't the first mistake of that kind, and sometimes one gets into real difficulties: which is the entity through which one will attempt the breakthrough? It was in many ways an ugly and unpleasant world with a singularly lethal atmosphere. I was glad to see the last of it.

One of the expedition—actually a younger son of my father, but by another mother, had an accident which resulted from a very slight fault in his insulation; by the time we got him back to the ship he was very ill. We thought for a time we wouldn't be able to save him, however we did. Miss Hayes was the leader of that expedition, and she had never lost a man yet.

He wanted me to let him father a baby, but I said no; the relationship was too close. I was worried enough about Viola, for it was clear that she had some of the delicacy one associates with haploidism, although she was as pretty as paint. Luckily my own heredity is on the whole good, but I did not like the way she got sudden headaches. And the thought of another close-up of genes worried me, though I felt I would like to have a baby, and to give a year to stabilising; I had plenty of material to work on which I could do at the same time. The father I finally chose was distantly related, a distinguished explorer for whom I still have the greatest respect; you would know his name. Perhaps I chose him almost too sensibly and deliberately; our son is intelligent and satisfactory, and may yet be as good as his father. My relations with both father and son are very happy. But I did not feel we should have a second child.

I was anxious after that to join the expedition which was going to clear up the problems of the grafts—or so it was intended. It had only just been realised by consulting all the old data from the first expedition, that the symbiosis worked out differently in earth conditions and on their original planet. It seemed important to clear this up. Pete Lorim was going as leader. Silis was elsewhere! Olga was intending to go as there seemed to be some interesting aquatic or semi-aquatic plants and she thought it might be useful to be able to reproduce for the grafts as much as possible of their home world during transplantation experiments on earth. But then she too found someone by whom she wanted deeply to have a child, so she decided to take time for that. However, she had a half-sister, who was also a very competent botanist, and who particularly loved getting things from one world to grow in another, though it is something one has to be very careful about for obvious reasons. Like Olga, Rima is sometimes tough with people but she is incredibly patient and delicate-fingered with plants.

As this was a world with a reasonable atmosphere, I had half a mind to take one of the laboratory animals, a Labrador bitch, Daisy was her name. Dear Daisy! She was the grand-daughter of the original Labrador, who had been one of the first experimental animals. Whether she had, in any sense, been "told" about the grafts is uncertain, but certainly something had been handed on; she had a kind of temperamental understanding of them. She was very like her beautiful grandmother. We had established a very good relationship and I thought I could explain to her some aspects of the work.

Then I ran into T'o M'Kasi again, quite by accident, in the restaurant of an airport where I was complaining about the fruit—they really might have it fresh there, of all places! Then he heard me and came over. I saw him against the flowers on the terrace and I wasn't interested in complaining any more, luckily for the airport chef. We started talking and I found his voice just the same. And his hands. We both missed our planes. He told me that the expedition he was preparing for was due to start almost at once, as soon as the checks were all through; one piece of faulty apparatus had to be replaced. I had to be quick. Not that there was any difficulty. No question of other choices this time. And before I knew where I was, I was in no condition to go on Pete's expedition.

I had, however, talked to them about the advisability of taking some of the laboratory animals, and finally Pete decided to take Daisy the Labrador, and one of the jackals, Kali, who was particularly quick and intelligent and another friend of mine. I was delighted about this, because otherwise, if I joined an expedition after my new baby, as of course I intended to do, I might never have seen them again, short-lived and time-bound as they were. It was most unusual to put members of other animal communities into time blackout. But these two, who had been brought up in a laboratory ambience, were different and could take in more human concepts. I gave them a preliminary idea so that, when the moment came, they would be at least co-operative. Normally the animal house technicians are non-exploring, cosy-box types; but one of them decided he would like to go with Daisy and Kali. He was in some way a badly integrated man, and he really wanted to get away altogether from his group—a different outlook from that of an explorer, but it seemed to fit in.

T'o and I came to the "tea-party" and saw them off. In a way I was half regretful. But not deeply. You may say I could have waited, but T'o was going on what was considered a dangerous piece of exploration; as a matter of fact he came back safe, but two others lost their lives. Anyhow there was a year of stabilising for another baby, three years of my life on Terra in the grip of time!

But I really had a delicious year, with my curly, coffee-coloured daughter and my blue-eyed toddler—so unlike her—beginning to talk and understand about numbers and distances and categories. And then there was little Viola, whom I could help to overcome her haploid difficulties and develop the talents which she could best use. Oh, I felt just like a twentieth-century Mum! I did everything. I sang and danced to them, I fed their measurements into the wooli-warm slots; I taught them to handle bees and spiders gently and understandingly, I stabilised them, I whispered to them the binomial and the basic equations and all that, when they were half asleep. I introduced them to their age group, withdrawing progressively as they became integrated. It must have been just like that in the old days, being a Mum. Only I could get away, that was the difference. How marvellous it was, in spite of tiny prickles of regret, to be back in a ship among my instruments and tables, thinking intently and uninterruptedly. And marvellous too, after thought, to go into meditation and out of time.

Yet somehow I have always felt a little closer to Viola. Integration for her could never be a hundred per cent complete. She still, I think, needs me a little, even to share her happinesses and successes. The physical delicacies could be overcome, but I always feel that, as her sole real parent, I have a double responsibility. The fact that Vly's accidental activation started her development made him a kind of parent, and has inhibited his natural feelings of revulsion towards a Terran female. Besides, he likes her small size. He has deliberately made opportunities to visit Terra, making sure that I would be there, and we have often seen her together. There is something about it all that makes me sure it is a plus fact in the great moral equation.

The next expedition, on which there were two Martian participants, was to a world of great beauty, but not altogether easy. The atmosphere, though not really dangerous, was thick, and the gravity was such that we found ourselves managing best with flippers and a semi-swimming movement. One had to accustom one's muscles to this. The bird-fish who were the main inhabitants screwed themselves along with a propeller-ish motion of glistening membranes. There was a long and streaming vegetation in a glory of soft colours. This opened and closed all round us, while the bird-fish, un-alarmed, screwed themselves past. The dominant species was rather like a dolphin, large brained and large eyed, but equally progressing with a corkscrew motion. We are well used to treating dolphins and dolphinoids as our intellectual equals, or, on certain subjects, superiors, so it was not too difficult to enter into communication.

The unfortunate thing was that we reminded them of a form of life which they had lately exterminated, one could understand why. It was difficult to get across very quickly that we were in fact something different. And they laid a kind of trap for us, something like an electric fence, only with a different type of power. It was one of the two Martians who was caught. In these circumstances there is always a psychological difficulty about a mixed expedition. The Terrans were in a way relieved that it was not one of themselves, though they tried to compensate towards the remaining Martian, who felt resentment and an enhancement of his normal repulsion towards humans. But again we attempted to overcome it, so that an artificial situation arose.

71

I was genuinely upset. I had got on well with the dead Martian, who was a relation of Vly—don't ask me to explain Martian relationships!—and I felt it was partly my fault at not being quicker on my communications. However, we did manage finally to get in touch with the dolphinoids. It is always easier when the fauna are on a recognisable scale. The real difficulty comes when there is, for example, some type of intelligence spreading thinly over an entire galaxy. Or again, when we just do not recognise the major forms of life—as on Jones 97.

As I became more skilled and practised, I was able to do more about this, though with some very remote forms none of us have yet managed to get on to communication. As you know, certain galaxies are not visited, and indeed we keep a rather careful watch on them. Even within galaxies where we have a certain contact, or where life has only occurred very sporadically, there are certain systems which we do not intend to visit yet. The time may come—I am sure it will—when we shall break through. I have one or two ideas which my group is working on, but much research and experiment is needed, and we cannot expect to get very rapid results.

One of the oddest of these worlds, all the more so as the answer was so obvious—once one saw it—came on a Minerals expedition. It was my first experience of the Minerals Ministry people, and at first I didn't find them congenial; they weren't quite like explorers; they were more obviously experts on one particular field and method, taking in whatever was useful to them from other scientific disciplines, but somehow without widely developed curiosity, man's supreme gift. However, they were doing a very necessary job on Minerals research, and gradually I got to like them. There was one man who had fallen head over heels in love with the screen image of my little Viola; by this time she had made quite a name for herself in the television games. I had done two expeditions since her birth, and, though it seemed a short time for me, it had given her time for growing up and success. Though would this be all? If she was really happy, I half hoped so, but she was still sub-adult. And when she was adult? During our last long-distance communication, she had giggled to me about some letters she had, very serious ones I gathered, and this Ministry man was the writer. I was careful never to tell him I knew, all the same. Viola is, of course, infertile, and perhaps this is just as well, because she would have been much too small to have a child by a human father. Her size did not seem to worry her at all at the moment. She was with a group of other young people, and I thought that she was probably not suffering at all because in one respect she was different from the others. That might have made things difficult at some points in Terran history, but by now we've got used to behaving politely to living entities of so many shapes and kinds that a mere difference in size is nothing.

During part of the time blackout on this voyage, I was in meditation, but my technique was not sufficiently developed and kept slipping off into nothingness. When I finally came back to full time and being, we were in orbit round a world which seemed to consist on its surface of evenly convex hills thickly wooded, or at any rate covered in some way. We could see no oceans, only occasionally a darkness which might be water between these round hills.

The mineralogists were already aware, through spectroscopic analysis and other techniques, that there were some very valuable materials in this world. You could see they were all on edge to get at them. The fact is we use up minerals too fast. We had a lot of arguments about that.

We made our landing space by the usual preliminary clearing technique, trying to give as much warning as possible to all fauna by means of uncomfortable but not deadly noise, heat and blast before the actual clearing. It was routine, but always makes me uncomfortable. We might unwittingly destroy some life which was not induced to move out by any of these stimuli, and of course we destroyed vegetation. However, one has little choice.

The atmosphere and gravity problem was not too serious, and the mineralogists, who always take far too little acclimatisation time, went scurrying off with a variety of clicking and humming machines which meant absolutely nothing to me, though I had become personally rather interested in one of them, a young man called Quinag—a smoothy, but what a delicious smoothy! I couldn't think what he was doing in the Ministry, but surmised that he might have misbehaved at some time. The man who wrote the letters to Viola could never have misbehaved.

Peder Pedersen was there too. It was, he said, his last voyage, and he had refused to come as leader, not feeling that he had any longer the necessary strength and flexibility. Our actual leader was that strange woman who called herself 513 because she had been one of the group that had discarded names—and indeed a great deal else. The Ministry trusted her, probably told her secrets; they were great ones for that kind of thing.

At first we did some straight old-fashioned exploring; I could find no species with which to get into communication, though there were some small forms scuttling mouselike or crablike through interstices of the thick growth which covered the hills, as well as some still smaller winged forms, often bright-coloured. The predominant growth was actually of three kinds. There was a tall, cylindrical, flexible growth which moved in a rhythmic way. After watching these for some time we realised that they had a very simple snapping head, two jaws—but were they jaws or toughened, thick leaves?—which opened and closed and occasionally caught one of the winged forms, whatever they were. There were somewhat thicker growths with feathery tops which waved and shivered; I felt that these were definitely
74

animal, to use a rather archaic classification, and was prepared to watch carefully before making any observations which would result in destroying or injuring one of them. And then there were curious and beautiful blunt-topped hexagonal forms, knobbed and striped and radiated in splendid colours. What were they? They were hard, rocky, perhaps, we thought, coralline. For a time we had been unable not to think of them as artefacts, as columns of some extraordinary temple, and yet that seemed improbable, especially as they seemed to grow out of the underlying hard rock which was only, as far as we could make out, covered to a depth of a few centimetres with dust and debris. However, it did set us off on to searching for some skilled intelligences which could somehow have made these columns. If we had found them they could surely have been communicated with! However, they excited our mineralogists extremely since it appeared that some of the brilliant colouring was due to traces of the rare mineral for which they were looking.

They immediately chopped off specimens and took them back to the ship, and excitedly discussed possibilities of large scale removal. 513 said dryly that we had better first find out what these objects were, what their use was, and to what or whom. It was just as well; even chipping off pieces as casually as they had done was a little bit unethical and worried some of us. We weren't quite used to the ways of the Ministry.

A little more exploration took us down the slopes to the edge of the dark, curving lakes round the bases of the great, rounded hills. There was no beach, only a thick clustering of the snappers which arched themselves into the top layer of the water—it was water, though with a number of minerals in it in heavy solution, and quite undrinkable. This top layer was packed with a life of a fairly low order; we took a number of specimens. There were mats of vegetation, mostly large, single cells strung together, but some a little more complex, any amount of material for our taxonomists who had a lovely time comparing all this with life-forms from other worlds in the same galaxy and elsewhere. The scuttlers, it was clear, had developed from an aquatic form, but probably found conditions safer beyond the top layer of water, though they sometimes came down into it to feed. But I didn't find any kind of consciousness with which I could possibly establish communication, still less anything which might have made the columns.

There had been some argument about getting down to the lake. We had to push or edge our way with some difficulty between the snappers, the featherd plumes and the hard columns. The snappers were perfectly harmless as far as we were concerned; there was nothing that could hurt even an ungloved hand. But the mineralogists, who were interested in bringing up large quantities of water for analysis, wanted to cut and level the way. Peder and I were against this. So, luckily, was 513, who finally told the Ministry people they must wait. When they grumbled about waste of time, she gave them a lecture on the nature of time which kept them quiet. Quinag meanwhile was occupied in seducing me. There is no more pleasing way of passing the odd half-hour when nothing more important is happening, and as there seemed to be no conscious life with which I could establish communication—though I kept worrying away at this, trying out and discarding various hypotheses—I thought I was quite likely to have quite a few spare half-hours. But I made up my mind that he would be a most unsuitable father; one does, after all, demand more than good looks and expertise. He had a second string in his own party, a girl called Soo, whose heart clearly was not in mineralogy. I thought she was a bit unadult for a space expedition.

We found ourselves increasingly with two interests. One group wanted above all to find out what kind of world this

76

was, what was the nature, reason for, and result of, these identical rounded hills, each of which—about this time we had made our way on to several others—had the same covering. We found our inflating boats perfectly adequate and pushed our way through the snappers. These were not hard enough to be more than a mild nuisance, even if they happened to catch one's arm or the blade of a paddle—the lakes were too narrow to make any kind of engine necessary—but we found they ingested pieces of malted bread with no trouble, and often used to feed them, especially if we wanted to quiet them while we made our own observations on the top layer of fauna and flora. I spent quite a bit of my time on this kind of thing, as I couldn't get on with my own job; still it always keeps one fresh to work within other people's discipline. There was an astonishing multiplicity of very small forms; we began to call them after one another, and then after all our friends.

We were in two minds about investigation of the snappers and feathery growths. They might have consciousness; one had seen forms as odd in other worlds; however, we did investigate those near the edge of our clearing; they seemed to have roots going deep down into the rocks. But there was no evidence of consciousness.

But the other group consisted of the mineralogists who, having satisfied themselves that the specimens of material which they had analysed were all that they'd hoped, now wanted to take back as much as the ship would hold. They were also evaporating out a good deal of the water. But it was the hard columns which really interested them. Some had been destroyed in the clearing technique for our landing, and most of the debris had blown away; as in so many worlds, there was a continual one-way wind blowing, not heavy, but never still. They cut down two or three columns near the edge, and found that it was only the first two or three centimetres down from the outside that interested them; most of the minerals were concentrated in the beautiful knobs and ridgings which differed slightly from one specimen to the next, though they were always more or less in the same general pattern. Inside the hard core was obviously of animal origin—but when? At what point were they connected with life? When would we, I thought, find a young one? Was there some obvious clue that had escaped us? That was what 513 thought, and said it was probably quite clear but we must continually change our focus: at some point the explanation would emerge. I kept trying to change my focus, but, while changing it, accidentally meeting Quinag.

Some of us tried looking in the upper layers of the water for any kind of fauna which could build up structures of this kind, perhaps in colonies. We found a few, but they were all minute and yet appeared to be adult; that was not the explanation. We were also watching for any regeneration on the cleared area of any of the forms. We did some experiments *in situ*, and found that the plumose type was a breather, though we could not see what it ingested. Gradually we all began to wonder if there was some connection between the three forms, especially when we found that where the mineralogists had taken a column, the snapper next to it began to droop and become inactive, and the plumose forms did not expand fully. And was this all? Peder Pedersen thought he had found some kind of tremor. The instruments corroborated him, though it was not very marked. I had not noticed it myself. We began to work out a theory of connections, but they would have to be below the level of the surface rock, or through the atmosphere; this latter seemed more probable and we set up various types of experimental interceptors. If the removal of a column was going to destroy or seriously harm the other forms, we would have to be careful about interference. The mineralogists, meanwhile, went on collecting, though Quinag was not in practice very diligent.

From the top of our own hill we could see all round, one

hill after another, all more or less alike, each divided from the next by a broader or narrower strip of dark, deep water. I was up there looking out from between two columns. I was feeling rather irritated, because this was a leisure moment and Quinag had gone away with Soo. I was saying to myself that this kind of petty resentment was most unsuitable for an explorer of my age and experience, but still I felt the pricklings of it. The snappers waved above my head. I began to concentrate and watch. I felt suddenly that I was on the point of realising what was what in this world if only I could see the connections more. I managed to shake off all thoughts of Quinag and concentrated still further. It seemed to me that something curious was happening. One of the further hills was very slowly rising, and at the same time two others seemed to sink. Perhaps, I thought, this had happened before but we had never stayed long enough to notice. One ceased to move; the others still seemed to be dropping into the sea, though it was difficult to be sure with these completely round and featureless objects all with the same covering. Yes, one of them at least was going down.

And suddenly I realised that this landscape of columns and snappers was exactly what one sees under a low power microscope looking at a sea urchin. These hills were simply enormous echinoderms.

I was caught with laughter. It was all so obvious. And of course so dangerous. The dark water had come up round that other hill, or rather the hill had sunk; it was only a small round island. But had these vast echinoderms evolved any kind of consciousness or intelligence? Could one get into any kind of contact? What stimulus made them rise and fall? What were they like underneath? How could one find out?

I went straight to 513. "Ah," she said, "that corresponds with the tremors." She showed me a couple of skeins of data with notes on the cutting down of the pillars. These were now being followed regularly by tremors, and the tremors seemed to be growing. "My own theory had been somewhat different, but I won't bother you with it, as I would suppose that our activities are beginning to get through to our hosts, who will probably delouse themselves. I'll call in the Ministry at once." She did that and explained our position. I estimated that the other form which I had seen sinking had probably taken an hour. But doubtless this could be accelerated. The tremors were now coming more quickly and regularly. We had better get everything into the ship, and be prepared to take off at short notice.

The Ministry people were very cross. They had not nearly filled their space. They reminded 513 of certain needs and promises. I couldn't make it out myself; they used the most stupidly round-about terms. 513 cut them short; her duty was to the safety of the expedition; she said a little coldly that we had probably been committing interference, which she would have to note in her report, but no punitive action would be taken if it were stopped immediately.

Quinag had edged close to me, and asked in a whisper if I didn't think it was nonsense. Wasn't 513 just being a bossy old mum? If they came back with a reasonable cargo, the Ministry had promised a bonus. It was surely unreasonable to talk about interference? He had the most distracting voice and way of touching, but I had suddenly thought of a possible method of communication with the entity under our feet. I said: "No, don't argue." That was the last thing I said to him. Because I dashed off to my instruments, and Peder came after me. Quinag wasn't interested, no, it wasn't at all his kind of thing.

There were two or three possible techniques of adjustment. I tried them all. At last I began to channel, and it was alarming. What I got was anger in extraordinary colours and shapes. I could scarcely take it, still less attempt to alter it. I could not get across to it myself. The colours and shapes convulsed, and there was a perceptible tremor under our feet. Peder said: "I think I shall help to pack up." He was swearing softly under his breath, the old Norwegian swear-words that I remembered from the Epsilon expedition.

I found the senior mineralogist still trying to argue with 513, but when I reported they agreed. I looked round for Quinag; he wasn't there, nor was Soo. We all got pretty busy, and then there was a further tremor, and someone shouted from the edge of the lake where they had been collapsing the boats. We were beginning to sink.

The zoologists came scrambling up, dragging the half-collapsed boat and the cases with their latest specimens. Our entity was sinking faster than the other one I had watched, and somehow I didn't wonder. The alarm was going out, and everyone crowding into the ship. Some equipment would be lost, but not more than one reckoned to lose in this kind of emergency. The navigators were all set. I saw the senior Ministry man with a great knob off one of the columns as big as he could carry. I was helping the zoologists; my own apparatus was all housed. We could see the water coming splashing up towards us, and the snappers eagerly bending forward to the lapping edge. There was nobody else in the clearing; the two zoologists were heaving up a last case; I hauled on it from the ship, then gave them a hand, and the lock slammed behind them. We dropped the cases into their wells and made fast. Vibration took over. "Positions for take-off!" came over the loudthinkers. We ran for our places and lay back, letting the couches take hold. And then the mounting stress, and then the weightlessness and the quiet. We could move again, and take stock before the time blackout.

There were, I remember, a few things broken, nothing

very important, but we had not stowed as well as we would have with rather longer warning. And then the senior Ministry man said: "Where's Quinag?" And he said it accusingly at me.

I said: "But he must be here!" For I couldn't believe he wasn't, and then I yelled across at 513: "Where is he? Didn't you check?"

She stood there very gravely and said: "He had exactly the same warning as everyone else; he should have been helping to stow. He was not doing so."

"Always a shirker!" said the senior Ministry man, half hysterically and still pointing at me—and of course I knew he hadn't approved.

513 went on: "There was no choice. We had to take off when we did. Not two seconds later."

"So you left him," the Ministry man said, "to drown!"

"To drown, I'm afraid," said 513. "Also poor little Soo."

I turned my face to the wall and cried without making a noise. You know how little room there really is in a space ship. I half heard Peder Pedersen speaking to the Ministry man. He came over to me after that and put his arm across my shoulders, strong and heavy, and old, so very different from Quinag's, but I managed not to mind. He said: "She had no choice."

"But she knew he wasn't back! On the check."

"She knew. She had to take the decision. I would have done the same if it had been my expedition. Luckily I never had to."

"Yes. It was his fault really."

"Certainly it was. I don't think he was the type for an expedition. And that poor little girl!"

"Yes," I said. "He probably wanted a last—oh Peder, was it partly my fault too?"

"Not very much," he said, "and there is nothing to be done but forget it. You'll try, won't you?"

But somehow one never completely forgets. Though drowning is a mild death for an explorer. Only he wasn't really an explorer. Not like Peder and me. Explorers are likely to have crueller deaths. But, being explorers, they know how to meet them.

CHAPTER SEVEN

Later on I had a child by Peder Pedersen, a blond son. He had only been a father once before, and his first son had been killed in an exploration disaster on his second voyage. He told me about that after the time blackout on our way back, when I was still considerably upset; it was good for me to realise what had happened to others. Material evidence had been collected later, and it was not the kind of death that one would like to envisage for any of one's children. In a part of his mind Peder was still uncomforted, though he could give so much comfort to other people. He thought he was not going to do any more real exploring, perhaps an occasional conference in our own galaxy, but nothing far-fetched. He would be a parent at hand for any of my children, and he would take Viola with him one day to visit her father. After spending a month or two with Peder I found myself wondering why there had not been a rush to choose him as a father. I think he had said no, probably more than once.

Meanwhile, there had been some mass grafting at the centre, and I was very anxious to know what had been happening about it. I had been away for some time in Terran years, and the handsome young man—was he 18 or 28, one can't tell once one is past adolescence oneself!—was Pete and Silis' child, Ket (trust Silis to give him a Changer's name!). Pete had been away for nearly 10 years, although no doubt it would only have taken a year or so of his own subjective time. Silis had been back for a while having another child—not by Pete, but by a topologist, who had been working on remote galaxy problems. It was clear she got on excellently with the young man whose mother she was! He told me all about the grafts, feeling perhaps that he was deputising for his father. I got the sense that Ket was somewhat over-identifying with Pete, possibly because of suppressed feelings for his mother. Rather enjoyable, though. We discussed Pete's plans at length; when he came back we would be able to prepare for much more far-reaching experiments.

It seemed that sooner or later all the grafts had died, not only my Ariel, and this had caused real grief, not to the znydgi, of course, nor to any male experimental animal, but in greater or less degree to the mares, jackal and dog bitches, and sows. A few Martians had volunteered, and were always thrown out of the bi-sexuality into female one-sexedness. They experienced grief of the kind I had known myself. Further, all the grafts had melted away on death, exactly as Ariel had done.

Further yet it had been observed that the hosts always became terribly thirsty, as indeed I had done myself, and when possible wanted to swim or bathe. But if they did the grafts always came away, deliquesced. The cell walls were apparently retained only for a few moments. The whole biochemical integration broke up. Two of the Martian hosts, for example, had gone swimming (so easy for them with the air pockets under the shells!) and lost their grafts. This led to further experiment. The mere splashing of water on the graft was apt to start a process in which its outer skin softened and its internal stiffening broke down.

However, most of the research effort had gone into what the grafts picked up from their hosts, and these were most odd. For instance, the grafts on the Martians had picked up an aversion to humans, especially human males, which the Martian temporary females had courteously avoided showing. Music was still the most easily transferred acquirement from host to graft. No other graft had repeated Ariel's demonstration of mathematics. But then, I said to myself, no other graft had been so much loved.

We had very little idea of when to expect Pete back. What with one unexpected deflection and another, space voyages of that remoteness were uncertain and likely to go on being so. Some day I suppose we shall be able to communicate instantaneously between galaxies. Or shall we? Well, the way isn't open yet, though some preliminary work is being done, much of it (but don't quote me!) singularly useless. Sometimes I wonder if I really want quite that amount of communications efficiency. Mightn't it take something out of exploration which we would miss, some spiritual tension that comes only in isolation?

However, I thought I had better put in time on another expedition myself. I had been tempted to stay at the immunological centre and even try another graft myself. It was odd how, once having experienced a graft, one felt two-minded about taking another; a mixture of attraction and repulsion which was too strong to be part of any normal make-up. The experimental animals had all felt it too, just as I had. Well, I must try again. I then began to realise that my intentions about the centre were not purely rational or scientific, not only in so far as the grafts stirred me up emotionally, but also because of young Ket. I began to realise that if I didn't look out I was going to commit interference between him and his age group. Of course this isn't forbidden by any code, but we all realise that it shouldn't be done.

I found that Miss Hayes was collecting an all-women biological group for a piece of exploration on a planet which distant probes had diagnosed as probably habitable, with a reasonable atmosphere, and certainly tenanted by life forms of some kind. Olga, who had satisfactorily stabilised her baby son, was going. Miss Hayes asked me to come as deputy leader; I said I wouldn't mind that. The whole thing seemed to fit into my needs. It turned out to be an extremely interesting expedition, and, as it ended by involving us in a fairly complex moral problem, I shall describe it in some detail. Meanwhile, I walked out on Ket and made a dash to say goodbye to Peder and Viola. Peder explained to me—and it turned out to be very useful—how to set up the most modern type of protective grid screen.

There was still no word of Pete when we took off. I hadn't been able to resist a last mid-distance talk with young Ket, and that before I changed out of my Terran flimsies into a decent space suit. Mid-distance shows up colours rather pleasingly! The voyage was quite uneventful; while we were on our near observation circuit, I thought of a possible new technique. I talked this over with Francoise, my junior on communications in this expedition; she seemed a very bright girl. But it would depend on molecular stresses, and, of course, one had no idea of what one might be trying to communicate with. There were two moons fairly close to this planet which had created a certain amount of navigation trouble, but nothing too difficult. It was touching to see how excited Nadira, our youngest member, was with her first expedition.

A piece of solid ground—that was what it fortunately turned out to be—which we had picked for our arrival was, as far as we could see, empty of any artificial or apparently artificial objects, and, of course, reasonably flat without major growth. It was not until we had explored into the edges among the clefts and growths that we found the race of inhabitants which, later on, we always called the caterpillars. Of course, this was nothing like their name for themselves, but it was some time before we established communication, though we could hear them bumbling away to themselves and one another, in what was obviously a form of auditory contact. Nor indeed was it the name we first used for them ourselves, for we had no idea of what type of life they were. The full grown ones were at least a metre in length, and at first we had equated them not so much with larval forms as with types of mature marine life. It was so clear that these creatures had some form of consciousness and intelligence that we could not consider making any anatomical observations. However, it is always such a pleasure to find genuine consciousness that one does not grudge extra time.

We did, however, observe their habits, especially when we were quite certain that the creatures were vegetarians. Their preference for damp, for wallowing in semi-liquid vegetable matter, especially the bogs of violet and purple algae, encouraged us in the marine supposition. Nor did we see any individuals of which these might be the larval form. Their breathing apparatus was not obvious, and they could disappear for hours in the damp depths of the algae, re-appearing with colour changes, often very striking—that at least was the only change that we could ascertain at first. These algal bogs were almost always to be found in the bottom of a cleft, and appeared to be very deep. We almost had a nasty accident in one of them. Above that level there were various types of vegetation, with or without what seemed at first to be chlorophyll, and occasionally of very great beauty. So that one could scarcely believe it: so that it blurs in memory. It was while I was investigating this that I was, as it happened, the first to get contact with the other form of life, though in a rather unpleasant manner.

We had by this time come to the conclusion that we had in the main to consider a non-vertebrate world; equally and rather to our surprise a non-flying world. There had been spider-like and crab-like forms, sometimes a little dangerous, and in the warm lagoons an extraordinary multiplicity of marine life which we were still working on.

Most of it seemed to be on a preconscious or at least pre-intelligent level, though Miss Hayes, who had more experience than any of us, was always warning us not to make hasty judgments. We had already collected a number of specimens and taken a mass of photographs and notes.

I was taking acclimatising time off with Olga. One cannot neglect this on an expedition, though some people can always be found to call it a waste of time. I always find it most productive of ideas. Olga was muttering excitedly about plants; luckily it was such an easy atmosphere that we could do without masks. Dear old oxygen, dear old carbon dioxide, dear old leaves! What had been developing here was an almost complete parallel with chlorophyll, and we felt quite at home as we went off together. Sometimes I almost envied Olga her single-minded curiosity. We thought we could manage a general look around with a bit of easy field botany thrown in. As we were scrambling about the clefts and uncertain of our handholds, we were roped. We had had quite enough of the bogs.

As far as concerns botany, I might, I think, manage to communicate the peculiar beauty of the flowers we found on the brim of the cleft. But it would take time. English would not in any case be the right Terran language in which to express it. The English have heaped so many overtones of emotion on to their own flowers—the dancing daffodil, the primrose by the river's brim, all the Shakespearean wildings, loveliest of trees the cherry—that they find it difficult to think in suitable terms even of the other wild flowers of bountiful Earth which happen not to flourish in English soil. The Japanese are just as bad. One might make the attempt in neo-Sanskrit. Let me merely say that those wavering and delicately winged blossoms were raising my pulse and respiration rate. Olga on the rope below me gave a kind of lion-like purr of pleasure and pointed.

I reached out my hand, and then for a moment I thought the plant itself had done something to me, had jabbed me with minute stings or prickles. But how? It appeared immobile. Then Olga screamed and pointed again. I saw something coming at me, a flurry of light and colour. I grabbed and broke a single blossom and tumbled down into the cleft beside Olga, who pulled down a great fern-like branch in front of us.

The stings and prickles which had been so nearly physical receded, leaving me instead with a horrible sense of guilt, not an adult feeling at all, not to be argued about, but overwhelming and seeking for punishment. Only when I found myself weeping, and a little sickish damp oozing out of my mouth and nose, and Olga shaking me, did I realise that I had been communicated with—"What were they?" I said, and she whispered back, "Butterflies. Only big butterflies."

That seemed to ease things a little. She stooped and picked up the flower, putting it quickly away in her vasculum; it did not seem to affect her, and I was glad it was out of sight. Otherwise I might have been compelled to try and restore it to its original place. Gradually the feeling of guilty misery cleared away. Now I only wanted to restore communication, even by pain, with whatever it was that had communicated.

Olga managed one photograph. When it was developed we went into conference over it. It looked as though this was a flying insect form which we had dismissed. It was Nadira, I think, who suggested first and rather shyly, because she was the least experienced of the team, that perhaps the caterpillars were—caterpillars whose adult form had at last appeared. But we had some hesitation about accepting this hypothesis, and we saw no more of the butterflies for some time.

Meanwhile we had made a good deal of progress in communication with the caterpillars. At first we had concentrated on the simple pleasure-pain complex. This was made easier when Francoise discovered that the creatures enjoyed being touched, at any rate in certain parts of their bodies. She was the one to develop a sympathy with them. I began to have great hopes of her; it looked as if her heart was in the job. It was her third expedition, and between whiles she had spent some time with my group, so I knew her fairly well, though perhaps Nadira, who was nearer to her in subjective age, knew her better. It is, of course, quite uncertain on any expedition which of a team will be the one to have this sympathy or empathy with other forms of life which we still tend to call "instinctive". But it usually happens, and is extremely important and useful. Francoise taught me how to handle the creatures to their satisfaction, thus making my work of communication much easier.

A great deal of their pleasure consisted in eating and evacuation. There was normally a good deal of waste cellulose in their food, which came out in pellets of several dark and shining colours. These formed the basis of quite elaborate pattern structures, which obviously gave great aesthetic pleasure to those who arranged and those who came to look at them. The caterpillars would caress these pellets with their soft blunted legs, and keep up a continual chorus of pleasure sounds, surrounding the successful artist with touch and apparently praise. We could ourselves see the interest of these patterns, mostly asymmetrical, but not without mathematical significance; deep blues and reds predominated, and the smell was not unpleasant. When they saw that we were interested, the caterpillars made room for us, and it was at these times we managed our earliest successful communications. Gradually we all came to like the caterpillars more and more, and to feel that this liking was reciprocated.

Francoise had thought this pattern making might have

some biological significance. Even under intimate inspection and handling, we had been unable to distinguish any sexual characteristics among these creatures, and this in itself suggested a larval form whose sex would only appear in the adult. Yet we could not be sure.

It was again Francoise who, through her sympathy with the creatures, arrived at some kind of solution. By this time we were managing a certain degree of communication on the "come—go: nice—nasty" level. Clearly, they realised we were friends, with some of the same interests as themselvs, not like the wood crabs which were among the carnivores and their special enemies. We used to take our rations and eat them where the creatures could observe us. This roused their sympathy, though they then wanted to see the results of the digestive process. I believe Françoise obliged, but they found the product aesthetically disappointing, and tried to express to her their pity and even some thoughts on how a better result could be achieved. This was a first important point of higher communication between our groups.

It was soon after this that Françoise realised what was happening in the bogs of violet algae, and that for a time put us off the larval track since it turned out to be a prolonged sexual wallow in which a number of individuals took part. The actual process was not clear, and it did not seem likely that the caterpillars were male and female in any direct sense. What resulted, however, was not only a curious type of fertilisation, whose significance became apparent later, but also a rise in temperature and a great accession of pleasure. We had by this time induced them to allow us to take an occasional blood sample, and it was then that we found, after the wallow and very much to our surprise, a general cell mitosis going on. The same individuals would go back several times for successive wallowing.

The caterpillars in their affectionate concern for Francoise wanted her to share this experience, and she would, I am sure, have made an attempt to join them but that our breathing apparatus was unsuitable for this type of work. However, our contacts were going very satisfactorily, and our note-books were filling, when events took another turn.

These bog wallowings normally took place when the two moons were up together; if we augmented them with our powerful ray torches more of the caterpillars seemed to come and they stayed under for longer. They ate heavily during the period of fertilisation, so that afterwards there was great aesthetic activity with the residue, which was more highly coloured than usual. Every piece of flat ground was covered with their patterns, or with the production of material for them. At the same time, the level of the bog was perceptibly lower after the caterpillars came out. We had not yet discovered the whereabouts of the next stage of reproductive activity, nor could we get any enlightenment about it from the caterpillars themselves, but I think we all hoped at any moment to arrive on some aspect of reproduction. We had never seen any caterpillars under eight centimetres long.

We were watching this gathering one night at the bottom of the cleft which, among ourselves, we usually called Wardour Street. Funny how much of ancient London has survived! We had a great feeling of sympathy and warmth towards the creatures, partly because we were all women.

We leant over and watched, the rays of our torches augmenting the moons. Françoise and Nadira were whispering; our recording and transmitting apparatuses were all at full adjustment. The caterpillars were wriggling in, the colours pulsating through the soft semi-transparence of their skins; their legs worked eagerly, their eye spots shone .Several of them got into happy communication with us. They did not resent the fact that we were there and watching them, in fact they seemed to welcome us.

And then wings were descending on us—or rather not

on us but on the caterpillars. We only felt the side-swipe of the feelings that were being projected upon the creatures. I recognised it as the same sense of guilt that had come on me when I picked the flowers, and my immediate reaction was of extreme resentment on behalf of the caterpillars, whose delight was shattered. One saw it from their behaviour even before communication came through: communication which was a pitiable crying for help, so that I thought suddenly and guiltily—a quite irrational and disquieting feeling—of my own little children, most of all Viola and my little curly-gold Jon, Peder's son.

The wretched caterpillars curled up or crept aside, the colours paled, the eye spots dimmed. They seemed to shrivel as from an inward searing. We watched with intent sympathy, not knowing whether or how to act ourselves. Yet we were also aware of the attackers, the whirl and flurry of wings, the colours beyond anything I have ever perceived on any planet of any sun, the antennae stiff and pointing like weapons of offence, the legs glittering and jointed as strange armour might have been. There were several of them, and for a moment one or another might be poised so that it could be seen, as doubtless it could see us from its flashing and faceted jewel eyes, now diamond, now sapphire or emerald. But it was beyond us what was happening, or why this anger and judgment was being projected on to the wretched crawlers in the bog of algae.

Two of the caterpillars had crawled right up to Francoise. She leant over and stroked and handled the poor things. I did the same when one came to me, but I noticed that my own hand was shaking. Even if one is not directly under it, such a torrent of blame is unnerving. And what had our poor soft friends done? There was a moment when it seemed to me that this was becoming intelligible, when I too began to regard the cowering unhappy creatures as somehow blameworthy. Then the contact fuzzed up, the wings lifted, the butterflies were gone.

CHAPTER EIGHT

We looked round at the caterpillars. We had wondered if
some of them were actually dead, but that was not so.
Those which had seemed stricken into complete rigor
slowly relaxed and edged away, their boneless legs scarcely walking. None of them went back into the purple bog.
Those which were nearest to us began to communicate, at
first in a formless misery and complaint, which gradually
turned into something more coherent which I could almost
translate into words: "Always, always they come when we
are happy, they stop us, stop happiness, why must they?
They hurt. They hurt. We are bad. They put out the light.
They burn into us. Pain. Pain. We were bad. They have
changed us, changed us. We will never have happiness
again."

Francoise and I communicated reassurance, yet we
wondered. Were our friends in fact changed? Would they
never be able to delight again in their multiple fertilising
wallow in the deep bogs? Had their masters been so fun-
damentally cruel as to cut them off from this? If so, why?
We felt we had to question our friends. We tried the
"why" question first. Did they know why this had been
done? The answer was a low moaning of guilt, yet clearly
they did not know what they had been guilty of. There was
only this feeling that they were "bad", but no knowledge
of what this could be. It was as though they were being
hurt from inside themselves by some unrecognised power.
Since they could not analyse themselves, we were only

97

hurting them worse by asking about it. Yet by now there was one thing above all which we had to find out about: what was the relationship between these two types of being? Could it be that our caterpillars were, in fact, larval forms of these butterflies? If so—but the question meant nothing to them; it could not be conveyed. "What happens when you are old?" I managed that. "We are shut," they said, "we melt up, we go." "And before you were here?" "We were little. The same but little. Our lives are all in one piece."

We tried another tack. We asked whether the invaders, for whom the caterpillars had a "word" with the feeling tone of "masters" or "pain-givers", ever came at any other time. "Yes, they come, they come, out of nothing they come. Suddenly they come. Always when we are happy, always they stop us. They stop us making patterns. They break our patterns. Always they hurt us, make us less. Sometimes they leave us for long, we forget them. We are happy. Always they come back. Help us, please help us."

It was difficult not to find this moving. We went into conference on it. Francoise had several of the creatures with her, in fact they would not leave her. We could see no physical damage on them, but they were obviously hurt; their colours were dim, they had no vitality; their communication with us constantly broke down into inarticulate misery. We all stroked them and tried to communicate; they did not, of course, understand what we were saying to one another.

One thing which we were deciding was that we must do further exploration. We had gone fairly slowly in a territorial sense. The earliest expeditions had wasted their energies and equipment on "exploration", whereas present tendencies are all towards acclimatisation and the kind of detailed knowledge of a locus which makes it "home". Thus, we ourselves had concentrated on intense study of a small area, and specifically on communication with the caterpillars, as also with one or two other species, though no other had developed sufficient consciousness for this. We had not attempted any physically difficult exploration, especially as we were not adapted to either the touch or the odour of some of the flora, which had quite an unpleasant effect on us. Miss Hayes and I had decided, when preparing the expedition, that we would not over-burden ourselves with transport equipment; one's space, after all, is limited, and even a light hoverer takes up a great deal. Also, of course, the interposition of any material substance between oneself and one's problem makes communication more difficult. However, now we must think again. If, as seemed likely, these creatures were larval forms of their attackers, we must try and find the intermediate stages: the egg, intermediate between butterfly and caterpillar, and the chrysalis or similar form, intermediate between caterpillar and butterfly.

Miss Hayes was the first to get up and leave the conference. She, as one of the older generation, had more the feeling for exploration in space; her empathy towards other species had been less developed. She had done more of the lagoon work of systematic classification. And she liked working by herself; it was likely that, on some future expedition, she would get herself into some position where she would die, equally alone, but making important observations. That would be her choice. How happy, if one's death coincides with one's death choice!

We did not expect her back for some hours, perhaps longer. The rest of us were concerned about the number of caterpillars that had come and put themselves, as it were, under our protection, and from whom we gathered that there had been further punishment from their flying lords and oppressors. We had decided that we must put up some type of ray-grid protection overhead, which might at least give reassurance to our guests, none of which were feeding. Luckily Peder had not only shown me how to set one up, but had also persuaded Miss Hayes to take the very newest type. We got it out, and Olga and I started feeding into the baby computer. It was rather fascinating to watch it adjusting itself.

Then Miss Hayes came back, to say that she had seen one or two specimens of the caterpillars which were clearly dead and being eaten by the wood crabs.

We were really upset. Poor soft, unhappy things! And what Miss Hayes had seen and we were all speaking about must, through its very vehemence, have broken through into communication which was, as it were, overheard. For the caterpillar beside me began to communicate in what was a surprisingly personal way. In general, theirs had always been a collective communication range. But this one seemed to be trying to express the thought that direct death from attack by the wood crabs was terrible but understandable. This death from the butterflies was not understandable, because not inflicted for food. The wood crabs were feeding now, but that was no part of the death intention. And a body which was not killed for eating should be shut, should be still, should be not seen. That was correct, as killing for eating was correct. But what had been happening was not correct. It was wrong, wrong, and now it was bound to go on happening, here or there. The masters, the punishers, they always struck blow after blow. When one thought they were away, back they came.

I explained the ray-grid as best I could, and the protection it should give. One of the navigators had begun picking up caterpillars and moving them under it. But my friend was uncomforted, weaved its head with the strange, prominent eyes to and fro. "I cannot stay with you," it said, "I must go—go far from you."

"But where?"

"I do not know," it said. "I become old. I must—I must—" And then its communication blurred out and it

100

began to move, stiffly, slowly.

"Stay under the ray-grid!" I told it, "you will be safe. We are helping you." But it was no use. My friend's head moved again, jerkily, and communication of affection and farewell came through. Then it humped its body, its legs gripped and it moved on, out of protection. "I'll go with it," I said, feeling oddly moved, "I'll keep in contact. This may tell us what we're after." As I went I saw that one of Francoise's friends, too, was leaving, coming the same way. Then another which had been lying half inert and coiled, joined us.

They went past their feeding places, then past several striking displays of pellets, without heeding. They went faster. They came to a thicket of sappy and tangled growth which I knew from past experience would have two unpleasant effects on humans. The leaves produced a nettle-like inflammation, and the smell, though not strong, produced vomiting, apparently by some direct nervous stimulation. However, the caterpillars pressed on through it, whether or not they felt either of these effects. So I was bound to follow them. I protected my face and hands as best I could and took a deep breath. However, the vomiting came on, and was so severe before I was through the thicket, that I found myself clutching blindly at leaves and branches so that the whole skin surface became inflamed. Luckily this did not last more than a couple of hours, but was distinctly unpleasant while it lasted.

Beyond the thicket there was a grove of large trees, of a kind I had not seen before, with straight drooping leaves. I kept from touching them, but later found they were quite harmless. Each of the caterpillars began to climb laboriously upward. I tried to communicate with them, but without result. I sat down, feeling weak and shaken, and watched them climb, then, slowly, drop themselves from the branches.

But, even as they dropped, they seemed to harden and

stiffen. I touched one: it was glued to the branch by its last pair of feet; there was nowhere about it the feel of the living flesh which, so short a time before, had enjoyed being touched and handled, the softness we had come to know so well. I adjusted my inter-communication set, got into contact with the others, and told them that this was it. We had the intermediate stage. I would wait but I had, of course, no notion of how long the chrysalid stage would last. I did not advise anyone else to come through the thicket, but, when I decided to come back, I would let them know, so that one of the others could be waiting at the far side with appropriate help. A second attack of vomiting on the scale of the previous one would be rather shattering.

Then for some time I wandered about in the wood. It was full of chrysalids, stiff and still and utterly silent. We had missed these trees earlier through avoiding the tangle. My face and hands were slightly less painful, though still swollen, and some stings had come through my clothing, especially round one ankle. I began to feel resentful at the thought of the various remedies at the camp which would have put it all right. And then I began to feel frightened. No doubt this was mostly the effect of the vomiting; I was thirsty but could do nothing about that either. But I began to be afraid of the silence. Again I got into contact with the others, but it seemed curiously unreal and unreassuring. Normally on an expedition one does not think about Terra or Terran relationships; it is distracting at a time when one must be single-minded. But now suddenly I found myself remembering Peder. Yet after the first small glow of comfort this too was unreal. What was increasingly real was the complete silence and these stiff, still bodies, each about a metre long, in a rigor of death-like change.

And then, suddenly, the silence ended in a tiny, ridiculous, popping noise, up on my left. I went over as quickly as I could, and watched the splitting of the dry old body which was now, so obviously, only a case or mask. Something was dragging out, apparently in pain, for it began to communicate almost at once. I could not pick it up at all accurately, nor was it, obviously, trying to get in touch with me; I was below it and it stared constantly up, dewed with a birth damp which dried slowly away.

It was, clearly, going to be a butterfly. It had the armoured legs, the beginning of jewel colour in the yet unbright eyes, and, hunched along its back, a crinkled greyish mass that seemed to be the main centre of pain and through which shivers passed continually. I so much wished that I could help it, as I could have helped it in an earlier life. At the same time I looked with great care for any sign of sexual differentiation but could make nothing out. And then another chrysalis began to split and more communication of pain and distress and need for assistance came throbbing out, affecting me with a fresh attack of vomiting, due to my feeling of uselessness and consequent contempt of myself. However, this was mild as compared with what I had gone through earlier.

At last the hatching creatures were answered. Down came the flurry and dazzle of wings, startling as ever, since the movement that brought them down was always the end of a very rapid zigzag. There were two butterflies over the first emergent creature, encouraging it, apparently, for it began to move more rapidly and its communication became less unhappy, more excited. The two butterflies concentrated on the wing mass, hovering over it, apparently, using claws and down bent antennae for unfolding, drying and soothing. Suddenly it became clear that the new butterfly was no longer in pain. Colours began to pulse and flicker through it; all over body and wings it stretched and hardened and brightened; the jewel colours flashed in its eyes. It looked at me, but did not seem even to recognise me as a living creature, potential enemy or

103

friend. I was so occupied in gazing at it that I did not see the beginning of the onslaught on the second emergent.

They were killing it, withering and blasting it, by no physical violence, but by the burning of their blame, which I could feel pouring by me. Hideous, inescapable guilt and disappointment (pure disappointment since it was for something not known) filled every morsel of what had once been a caterpillar. It lost confidence, lost all will to be born and live. It died. Then I saw that its wing mass was uneven. If it had lived, it would have been with a crippled wing. But it had not lived. Not at least in its new life.

I stooped over it, partly in pity but mostly in order to take measurements and make notes. I was particularly interested in its feet, for it seemed to me that the first pair had developed, as I had suspected from watching the butterflies at work, into claws with sensitivity, which must mean some unarmoured portion, usable for manual purposes. Then suddenly came the wood crabs and I got out of the way quickly; they had not attacked any of us observers so far, but I disliked their methods. Now I saw that the new individual was about to take flight and that the others, having finished their murder, were encouraging it. They swayed the branch that it was on. It hesitated, flickered, suddenly heaved itself and flapped. I got the tail end of a sensation of astonishing joy that, had I experienced it fully, would have been unbelievably beyond anything I have ever known. Although I have known, and I hope shall know, much joy. It was not only the delight of the new movement, of light after darkness, life in a superb form, but also it seemed to be a sense of justification, almost of complete virtue, yet of a pure virtue with no origin, no intention. The other butterflies whirled up with it. Then, one of them dropped back and came towards me.

I was taken aback, almost frightened. I had been so much on the other side. Was this enemy creature about to try and treat me as if I were a caterpillar? I knew I was weakened with vomiting and pain. I had brought my weapon with me—this thing which I had never, in all my expeditions, actually used. Was this the moment to have it ready? I admit I was afraid of the butterfly. Yet at the same time my curiosity, which has so often saved me in moments of exploration emergency, was stronger than my fear and I waited, trying to attune myself, trying to note the rhythms of colour change in the butterfly's wings and eyes, but failing, this time, to find them.

Its first communication seemed again to be one of blame, and I thought it was equating me with the caterpillars; yet it was not so strong, so absolute, as the blast on them. There was a kind of twist in it and that was what I had to understand. If the butterflies had made any kind of sound, it would have been easier, but this was an entirely beamed communication, not broken up or analytical or concerned with objects and actions, but expressing complete emotional and, I was beginning to think, intellectual states. What was coming through now appeared to be an emotional state of blame for my thoughts or intentions, but mixed with an intellectual state of understanding or even explanation. It seemed to be demanding of me a contrast between the newly emerged, living and joyful butterfly and the wretched dead one, and then a realisation that the dead one was dead because of something in its own nature. And for this, blame, blame, blame!

I tried to respond with as complete a state of feeling or thought as I could manage, on the lines of pure intellectual curiosity, but it was not easy. I was reassured to discover that the butterfly seemed to be comprehending my difficulty, if with impatience. It was not, in any sense, a direct enemy. Its antennae quivered, and its eyes changed colour rapidly. When it turned this state of impatience on to me, I felt quite ridiculously churned up and unable, as it were, to get in a word—or a state—edgeways. Whatever their method of communication, it had tremendously strong direction and impact. Suddenly the butterfly bounced into a zigzag and disappeared, leaving me with a sense of loss which, later, I came to associate with their rapid departures.

In this mild misery, and wishing I could have a dose of alcohol or caffeine or some similar stimulant, I wandered back to the tree in which my first poor friend now hung stiff and presumably changing. I saw at a distance another hatching, but could not get there in time. It must have been a quick and joyous take-off. I also found a half-eaten cripple, dead, doubtless of blame.

Had these new butterflies any remembrance of their earlier state? It seemed to me highly doubtful. Any kind of mnemonic organisation, for obviously memory always depends on some biological order and pattern, in whatever species, must have been disorganised completely during the change from one kind of being into another. And now I began to wonder about the cells in the caterpillars in which post-wallowing mitosis had taken place. Was there being a complete cytological breakdown, or did the individual cells persist? I could get the evidence, I thought, from the half-eaten specimen. It was odd how reluctant I felt, in my then state, to touch it.

I stood there with my hand on the chrysalis of my old friend, who would obviously never recognise me nor wish to communicate with me again. My sadness was only broken when signals began to come through from the others, saying that the caterpillars were on the move in my direction, and that, if they made for this wood, either I should make the effort to come out, when everything would be ready in the way of remedies, or else Miss Hayes would come through and bring me help. I said I would make the effort. There was no point in doing anything else. We could no doubt have used means of destroying some part of the evil thicket, but this would be against the fundamental policy of non-interference.

I waited until the first of this batch of caterpillars were coming through. I stroked them, and they responded feebly and affectionately before climbing their trees and settling into what, for them as they were, was equivalent to death: might be death indeed if their development was not considered adequate by their masters. Then I went back through the thicket. It was extremely unpleasant, in fact by the last step into the open, I was barely conscious. I opened my eyes again with my head on Olga's knee; I was staring up at the familiar scar across Miss Hayes' cheek as thought it were something of great significance, as perhaps it was: a symbol of noble biological curiosity. The nausea and pain were standing away from me; soon I could get on to my feet.

What followed was a long and interesting technical discussion on how to break up the communications from the butterflies into something intelligible for ourselves, that is to say, on the whole, statements with implications of opposites, not the complete synthesis of these conveyed states of theirs. It would, we thought, need some co-operation from them. We ourselves must try to simplify and synthesise our own communications.

Meanwhile, how little of the old happy caterpillar activity there seemed to be! No making of art forms, no wallowings. We did, however, see rather more of the smaller younger caterpillars, but they seemed to do little communicating, even with one another, and their activities seemed unco-ordinated. Had the older ones been able to pass on to them the legend and terror of the descending butterflies? Had they been warned?

Francoise was extremely depressed; she had become more involved than any of us have a right to be. After all our experience in space exploration, we from Terra ought to know better than to let our soft hearts go over the problems of another species or another completely alien form of life. Yet that is exactly what we do, time after time.

Francoise used to go and cry over the old patterns of excrement which were now drying up and blowing about. Nadira used to go with her sometimes and sympathise, as did one of the navigators. Miss Hayes sent off on long expeditions, in the course of one of which she lost the top joint of one of her fingers. Olga was writing notes. She found it best to get her botanical specimens by night, as during the day she was more likely to be attacked by the butterflies. She was much the least susceptible of any of us to their communication of anger and blame, but even she tended to find them oppressive. Meanwhile I myself was working solidly on the communication problem.

Luckily my opposite numbers on the butterfly side had been working along the same lines. But indeed it was not a matter of luck; as far as I can make out, we had the only solution. At any rate our co-ordinates agreed.

We were all there, as it happened, when the butterflies came down. Francoise had brought along two half-grown caterpillars and was fondling them. They had just started elementary pattern-making, and she was feeling a little cheered up. When Olga pointed and shouted, she picked up the caterpillars and threw her arms over them.

There were two of these butterflies, one of which was predominantly in patterns or rhythms of red which tended sometimes to disappear into a kind of grey—and yet that is not the word for it—which was difficult to look at, giving one a kind of visual shock. Presumably it was an infra-red colour which we could not see. I found this both with the predominantly reds and also the predominantly blues, where one had the same experience with the ultra-violet. The other butterfly was in the middle hues of the spectrum.

They began to communicate in what one might have called speech had it been in the auditory range. Or rather, the red one did this for me, after certain adjustments, but the other was occupying itself by throwing down a blast of blame on to Francoise. I was so interested in this opening up of the closed circuit that I did not even notice, until Francoise yelled. I had no idea of how thoroughly the old gutter argot had survived, at any rate among ex-students of the Sorbonne. Even the butterfly was for a moment checked by the intensity and single-mindedness of her emotional state. Then it started again.

We had a small section of ray-grid still in place, and Olga dashed to the computer for more, while Francoise ducked under, holding her caterpillars, and, regrettably, spat. Obviously the ray-grid did not completely protect her or her caterpillars from the butterfly. I could see them writhing and curling up, and managed to convey to the red butterfly that this must stop before we could go on communicating.

I shall now try to put into sentences the substance of our communication, all, of course, from notes taken at the time by each of us separately and then collated; we did not all get the same sense and occasionally the whole thing became uncertain, nor do I think our own communications were always intelligible to them. Later on we both improved things. The butterflies had obviously meant to begin in some other way, but they were deflected by Francoise and her caterpillars. "Why does it protect them?" they said. "It is wrong."

I said: "We all want to help them. They are soft, they are sad. Why must you hurt them?"

"They must be hurt," the butterflies said. "Hurt. Punished. Then they will not do these things. These wickednesses."

"Why do you want to stop them? It is part of their life. One day they will be as you."

The butterflies did not like it when I expressed that; the vibrations jarred; and yet it was something they knew. Then the red one expressed itself carefully, and with distaste apparent: "What they are makes what they will be. They make us." I agreed. The butterfly turned fierce and quivering antennae on Francoise and I got the feeling, subsequently confirmed, that these antennae were highly directional, could concentrate the emotional communications. "It holds them," the butterfly said. "It helps them to do wrong. It helps them to make patterns!"

"Why must they not make patterns?" I asked.

The red butterfly did not communicate for a moment, and the other one darted angrily over the ray-grid. Then the red one said: "If they do that thing, then, when they become alive, the wings—" Here the communication blurred. "The wings—are hurt. Wings—do not come."

So this was perhaps the explanation of what I had seen. "Why?" I said. Both butterflies began to communicate, and it was difficult to disentangle, but I managed to gather then, as we confirmed later, that pattern making involved—or at least that was their theory—a concentration of energy and interest on the visceral parts as opposed to the area of future wing development, and the externalising of a rhythm or pattern that should—again according to the butterflies—be internal. It was then that I suddenly realised that the rhythm of colour in the wings of the butterflies was comparable with, though more complex than, the excremental patterns of the caterpillars. It seemed that the butterflies hoped that the caterpillars could be driven into conserving and internalising these rhythms, and that one of the things they most hated was the great displays of pattern-making such as we had seen at first, and which had been the beginning of our real contact with the caterpillars: in fact, the first activities which had aroused empathy in Francoise and then in the rest of us.

We had no means of knowing if the butterflies' theory was correct, and felt that it would require anatomical observations to check on it. But it did explain some of their certainly Francoise, who, after all, had not seen the half-winged emerger from the chrysalis, simply did not believe

110

them. She tired to say that they merely wanted power, and had invented this story to justify themselves, but, fortunately perhaps, did not manage to convey it, except as a complete state of disbelief.

Suddenly one of the butterflies communicated again, obviously about her: "It stops us from telling. It hates. We will come again." And they whirled away as quickly as they had come.

This left us plenty to discuss and we began, uncomfortably, to find ourselves taking sides. Miss Hayes found the butterflies a most interesting form of life, a possible intellectual stimulant and contact. Francoise said coldly that what they had put across was impossible, and untrue. She could feel the cruelty and hatred behind these ideas. She fondled the two small caterpillars who unstiffened a little. "Pattern-making is their highest form of activity and happiness," she said. "We cannot desert them. At any rate, I cannot."

Nadira was with her over this question of loyalties, yet had the sense to realise that they were both taking a somewhat unscientific point of view. The navigators were worried and uncertain. So was the geologist, who didn't want to think about it. Olga laughed and teased the rest of us. I myself only wanted to continue with the communication and to work out better methods. Besides, though I had been in sympathy with the caterpillars, not the least in their wallowings, I felt that the essential, now, was to be reasonably objective. It did, however, occur to me that the peculiarly violent tensions which had developed among us might have been somewhat eased if this expedition had happened to include one or two men.

It was some days before the butterflies came back. And certaily n Francoise was encouraging the young ones, which were growing quickly, to make patterns. In fact she was going beyond her duty of sympathy into something very near interference. It worried Miss Hayes and me: what ought we to do?

I was with Olga, mending and testing a piece of equipment and discussing a few details of the return voyage. The butterflies swooped down on us in a superbly accurate side-slip. Communications began almost before we could get ready. They were now bent on explaining the other way in which the caterpillars appeared to be especially blameworthy. This involved the wallowings in the algal bogs and took some time to get across, as much of this was so important to the butterflies that they could not bring themselves to analyse or break down their direct states of feeling about it. Nor did their impatience when I failed to understand make things any easier. What it came to was that these generally fertilised caterpillars were reborn as butterflies which would sooner or later have to lay eggs. The process of egg-laying invariably killed the butterfly, not only through physical stress, but also through knowledge that it was now doomed to pass on life through tens, perhaps hundreds—I could not get the numbers at all clear—of these lowly forms, most of which would inevitably commit wickedness after wickedness and so never attain a state of bliss.

I tried to suggest that, if no eggs were laid, not only would there be no caterpillars, but also no butterflies. This was brushed aside. It was conveyed that very occasionally an unfertilised caterpillar—probably driven away by butterfly attack from every attempt at bog-wallowing, discouraged to the point of going into chrysalis form, but not actually killed—would in due course hatch out into rebirth. If it had also been discouraged from pattern-making and had perfect wings, there was no reason why it should not live for ever. The butterflies had, as far as we could see, no natural enemies. Nor were they affected by the seasons, such as they were in that particular planet.

It was difficult to find out about disease or, for that

matter, wear and tear. But it seemed that every one of these actual few non-egg-laying individuals was living, and in a state which my informants found it impossible to convey, except that, if a butterfly flits over the lagoon, there is the butterfly and there is the reflected butterfly. The state of these individuals, as compared with that of the others, was like the butterfly itself.

It took us at least two hours to arrive at this. At the end they darted away, leaving us both with the disconcerting sense of loss, yet they returned very quickly and then all at once plunged into the matter of the flowers. We had already observed that there were some flowers out of which they extracted not, as far as we could make out, any kind of nectar, but the scent itself. Others were used in a kind of rhythmical game or dance in which they sometimes became involved. It was impossible to tell whether there was an element of aesthetic enjoyment in all this, though it did seem to be that certain of the loveliest colours and shapes were as attractive to the butterflies as to us. Any interference with the flowers was thought to be blameworthy, not quite in the same way as the caterpillars' activities, but meriting a sharp attack. This was partly physical in its effect because it was used to ward off some of the other forms of insect life, which might have damaged the flowers, but which were perhaps not susceptible to the state of total blame which was their other form of attack; hence the purely physical pricking sensation which I had experienced myself.

The red one wanted to know why "It" had picked the flowers. I explained that Olga only wanted one specimen of each and wanted it to think about, and that she was preserving them carefully. I realised with some difficulty that they wanted to see this. Olga got out one of our best specimens. Naturally, with the problems of packing all our material into a quite restricted space during transport back, it was not in Museum condition. I found it impossible to get them to understand the further processes which would take it back into something approaching its real beauty.

Both butterflies became extremely agitated. They felt, I think, that Olga had taken, not merely the flower, but its colour, texture and scent. Every now and then both sent out a shower of prickles which I disliked more than Olga did. I tried to soothe them with the concept that this uninviting object could not only be restored, but would be used for purposes of knowledge and admiration. But it was hard to make out what was getting through in the state of agitation the butterflies were in. Suddenly they turned and shot away with wing flaps too rapid to be visible; in a moment they were out of sight. "Well!" said Olga, and shook herself like a dog coming out of water.

CHAPTER NINE

The usual minor navigational difficulties about our return were having to be solved, as such comparatively mathematical problems normally can be solved, given the right effort and equipment. But the feeling that the expedition was divided in mind, and perhaps even in object, was not at all pleasant, and limited the cooperation which was vital at this stage. Francoise spent all her time encouraging a group of young caterpillars which were growing fast, except for the few which had been permanently damaged, and on which she seemed to us to be lavishing a quite irrational amount of care and affection. As for the rest, she said, rather defiantly, that they would soon be at the pattern-making, and then the bog-wallowing stage. I was considerably worried about this, especially as I had been visited two or three times by the butterflies, and had managed to clarify certain points. But Francoise seemed at the moment to be immune to ordinary argument and reason. One of the navigators, who had turned out to have quite a flair for our type of communication, was strongly on her side. Miss Hayes now went off on an exploration of her own, partly, I believe, in order to think all this out, and it was while clambering around in the far end of one of the clefts that she accidentally found one of our missing clues.

She told me afterwards that she had attributed the sense of grief which was gradually beginning to overwhelm her, the further she went, to worry about the expedition and to fear that Francoise's present irrationality might spread to other subjects, and could easily make the take-off more difficult and dangerous, not only to ourselves but to our specimens. Yet normally this type of worry would have induced her to take mental action at least. Now it was becoming more and more oppressive, jerking her back to Terran experiences which she had long sublimated and which, in the ordinary way, she could recollect with calm and often enough amusement. Now they weighed her down; she felt a sense of irreparable loss, as though she had suddenly realised that her whole working life had been a dream. At some point, it seemed, she had taken a wrong decision: nothing afterwards had any value. So strong was this feeling that she had almost stopped observing, and in this state she very nearly walked into the source—as she realised with the kind of relief that comes with waking out of nightmare—of all this storm of grief. It was, of course, a butterfly laying and dying. The enormous and beautiful something which we knew was normally revolting to the butterflies. Its antennae drooped, its sensitive claw feet gripped and relaxed, gripped and relaxed. Shudders of colours, broken rhythms, went through its wings, and the eggs poured out, tearing its body and leaving a trail on the algae which gradually sank, not perhaps to the bottom, but at least below the surface. It was difficult to be certain whether or not it was in pain as we ourselves and many other Terran and extra-Terran species know such sensations. What it was sending out was waves of grief and discouragement of the deepest kind.

As soon as she was aware of what was happening, Miss Hayes tried to contact it with compassion. Yet perhaps pure compassion is too human a thing: it did not appear to be effective. Though this occurred to Miss Hayes it might yet not be the whole story. She began to think that belonging as she did to a slightly older generation than the rest of us, she might not be quite up in the latest techniques of communication; it seemed possible that I or one of the others would be more successful. She sent out a general call for the rest of us, and we all hurried to the place she had indicated. Here at last was the link we had not yet found.

Olga and I happened to be the nearest, as we were making some botanical and ecological observations. When we arrived and found ourselves in the area of grief, we too attempted communication, but it seemed impossible. In an older day maternity must have been equally painful for Terran mothers—if, that is, the pain of torn tissues on one planet can ever be equated with those on another. Yet these mothers always had the feeling of pride and achievement and creation which to some extent overcame the pain and fear. With them it was a beginning of maternal feelings; active pride would turn into passive patience, creation into solicitude towards the thing created: something near our present-day feelings.

But the butterfly had no maternal feelings, could not have. It was no part of this evolutionary pattern. The eggs would look after themselves, even if a few perished; and when they hatched it would be into something utterly alien from their mother, and, again, capable of survival on their own. Maternal feelings could have had no outlet. The butterfly's egg-laying then was pure loss. Nor could we convey to her that she was in any way continuing life, was part of some process which we did not try to explain, only to communicate as some kind of consolation.

The butterfly seemed feebler; the colours in her spread palpitating wings were less bright. She did not appear to see. Only a few eggs were now emerging from the dreadfully torn end of the ovidect—or was it a real oviduct? Perhaps it was simply a way torn and blasted through the tissues of the abdomen by sheer physical pressure. We would, we hoped, be able to investigate this later. How many eggs had been laid? Miss Hayes did not know for certain because by the time she had arrived the process was well under way. Probably the first laid eggs were already below the algal surface. However, one could make a guess, given the size of the eggs and the size of the butterfly, at some number above fifty and below a hundred.

Nadira and Francoise had now arrived on the scene. Francoise said little, but from what she did say it was obvious—and to me rather curious—that her compassion towards the caterpillars did not extend to the equally suffering butterfly. While we were still watching rather unhappily, since it was impossible to escape from the area of grief and it affected us with memories and foreboding, even though we knew it was nothing to do with us except as fellow animals, something else happened. Three other butterflies swooped down in their blinding zigzags, giving out signs of intense disturbance.

I wondered whether they were being able to reach their dying friend, who had now almost ceased to lay, with any sort of help; if so it was impossible to pick up its nature, which may well have been of an intellectual rather than emotionally compassionate kind, not as it were "beyond" us but out of our focus. I thought I sensed a difference in the tide of grief, a change of attitude almost; it was not easy to get it straight, however, because I had become occupied in deep and irrational grieving for the death of my own father—a most illogical thing to do which in the ordinary way would never have occurred, since I was proud and happy about my father who had chosen to undertake an interesting and successful piece of work of a kind which was incompatible with the continuation of human life. But now his remembered face was a centre of grief. Then, equally strongly, I remembered my mother, and imagined with terrible vividness how she might have felt about me, her child—always, to her, her little, loved child—in the moments before her ship burst open and all in it exploded into the enormous, lonely emptiness between the galaxies As I thought of them both, I could feel tears running down my face, and saw that Olga, of all people, was equally affected. She told me afterwards how she too had thought of her dead mother—her father, an administrator, was still alive.

When I had extricated myself from this strange personal shadow, I was suddenly aware of a change in the dying butterfly, which seemed to be in contact with the others, since its antennae were raised. The grief was changing in character, etheralising perhaps. Then Francoise cried out, "Look!" and we saw that an attack was going on upon the most recently laid eggs. This seemed to be of the physical type which Olga and I had experienced when picking flowers. The semi-transparent egg capsules shrivelled as though in intense heat. With some difficulty I reached across the algal bed, not sure how deep it was here, and picked one up. The contact was momentarily stinging, but I brought it and a few others back. There were plenty of anatomical and biochemical data which we still needed.

Then Francoise shook herself angrily; the butterflies had apparently recognised her and were assailing her with blame—this was what came of defending the wallowings of the caterpillars! Immediately she got into a fierce feeling-entanglement with them, contrary to our whole ethic of non-interference which she, of course, like all the rest of us, had agreed to whole-heartedly before coming on the expedition. Luckily she and they were both too agitated, for different reasons, to be able to communicate. Also, and equally of course, I managed to do some jamming, not wanting trouble. But how stupid it all was! And, partly no doubt because of the way the cloud of grief was affecting Francoise, I guessed—and on questioning her later it turned out to be correct—that it had set her off on thinking about her damaged and miserable caterpillars. Her children. She had not yet had any babies of her own.

Then suddenly the grief was switched off. I began to

119

feel in balance again. The butterfly had died.

It was very curious: the colours in its wings became blurred, static and in an odd way ugly, like a badly designed carpet or curtain. Nor was there the same subtlety in the tints and shades. We all felt a kind of embarrassment, especially as we hoped to be allowed to take away the body. But would we be able to do so? The butterflies which were now zigzagging above us were not those we had communicated with before, and did not seem able to pick up anything about our intentions from me or the others. However, in a short time the predominantly red butterfly, with which we had developed communication to something approaching speech level, came to join the first three. We managed to explain that we would like to take the dead body of their friend back to our camp. It had the most unforeseen effect. The butterflies flew into a passion of anger and resentment, and after a moment I was able to arrive at the fact that they were identifying us with the wood crabs.

It was no use getting upset, of course; I tried to convey that it was out of admiration for the beauty of the butterfly that we had been moved to make the request, but perhaps I could not entirely keep out the scientific interest. At any rate, the answer was that we wanted to absorb it, to take it into ourselves, in fact, to eat it, and they could not allow this. It was hideous and horrible. This butterfly, it seemed, was not thought of as they had thought of the emergents whom they had so casually blasted and left to be eaten. This was one of themselves struck by a doom which perhaps they themselves would not escape. This butterfly had danced over blossoms in their own perfection. It was part of themselves. Reluctantly we had to acquiesce and watch them lift and take away a whole body of unsolved problems to some destination which we could not guess at. "The caterpillars get eaten by wood crabs!" said Francoise bitterly, "and those butterflies couldn't care ss!" She seemed unable at this stage not to make a personal matter of everything.

"We had better scrape off the surface of this," said Miss Hayes, trying the edge of the algal bog with her foot, "and see if we can get some live eggs."

"No!" siad Françoise, "how can we be their enemies too?" But Nadira managed to calm her down and bring her into a more rational frame of mind. Probably a good many centuries of Indian respect for life, which is of a quite different kind from the European—they are often mutually unintelligible—coupled with a biological training which induced another type of respect, had ended by making Nadira a more civilised person than Francoise, whose ancestors had been soldiers and steak-eaters, passionate takers of sides and of live. Such matters of history have their effect.

We found that the bog at this point was not deep, and we managed to collect a number of eggs. It might be possible to guess from their development when they would be likely to hatch. That evening we managed a great deal of fascinating work on them, most of which naturally went into our report. Yet Francoise was still hanging back. It would have been interesting to know if the butterflies at all realised beforehand what was going to happen to them, whether egg-laying came upon them suddenly, whether there was any possible preparation, emotional or physical. If a very high percentage, including probably those who had attended the death, were going to have to go through it themselves—inexorably—it would account for the violence of their attacks on the bog-wallowing of the caterpillars. At what point did a butterfly know if it was one of the unfertilised minority? Or did they all keep on hoping up to the last?

We discussed this on and off for the next few days. In a way it was like the earlier days of Terran life, when people did not risk their lives as deliberately and intellectually as

we explorers do, but were liable to be killed by some pain
ful and complex tearing or destruction of tissues com
parable with this one which we had witnessed on another
planet. That too, must have been cause for grief and
resentment and anger.

Then the two butterflies with which we had first com
municated came back with their usual abruptness and in
sistence on immediate sensitivity to themselves, whatever
else we might be doing. Now they were simply and solely
at us to come, come, come with them. They were im
mensely agitated, but with a pleasurable agitation. They
did not even spark at Francoise.

We scrambled along after them. It was rather hard
going. They took us through a thicket of some of the
singularly unpleasant plants which, like those outside the
grove where a chrysalis hung on each tree, stung any un
protected skin and at the same time produced a feeling of
nausea. It was while we were still in very great discomfort
from this that we began to experience something al
together new.

This begins to be extremely difficult to describe, except
in analogy. But it resembled the dream which I believe
most Terrans have in which it has at last become apparent
that all problems are ludicrously simple and solvable, once
some principle is grasped: that complete and eternal hap
piness and knowledge are within easy reach. It is, of
course, a negation of the human condition, though some
thing to which perhaps we have struggled a little way. The
elements of this feeling, then, were unswerving optimism
based on almost arrived-at universal perception and in
sight. Our nausea and pain had vanished in this glow of
happiness or, in so far as they were still there, were unim
portant—as unimportant as the tickle of an old scar to
someone listening to the climax of some superb piece of or
chestration. "You are near," the butterflies signalled to us,
"near." And somehow we were certain—or at least I

was—that they shared whatever area of feeling we ourselves had gone into.

It was curious that none of us noticed the other butterfly until we were almost on it. I suppose we had expected some still more astonishing play and blaze of colour. In fact it was almost colourless, though the rhythms of colour still played through the greys and creams, the dusk and early dawn, of its wingspread. It was circling round a tree which had a particularly beautiful and curiously shaped blossom; once it alighted apparently to find a more intense aesthetic perception whose echoes reached me as an enhanced sense of well-being or hope. I could see Miss Hayes smiling to herself as she accepted it, and Olga a bit disturbed, since she herself had looked at the flowers in a somewhat predatory way.

The red butterfly was communicating, telling us that here was one who had escaped from the common doom. I tried to find out how old it might be, but clearly the red one did not know. I sat down on a rock; there seemed to be no reason at all for going away—ever. What state could be better than this? Miss Hayes and Nadira both sat down, and then Olga with the two navigators, one on each side of her. I cannot be sure how long we were there, but suddenly I found myself shaken by Francoise.

Her face was twisted and redly suffused with effort. "Come away!" she said. "Come away! Remember what they *do*—the pain!" It was apparent that she was struggling against the sensations of happiness or peace, and I felt, out of my own happiness, that I must help her, if necessary by breaking away from it myself. I ceased to allow communication with the butterflies. Perhaps indeed we had experienced enough for our purposes of understanding and subsequent report. Any more of this bliss might have had some demoralising effect on us, making us less able to think or act in a fully intelligent way. Francoise was speaking now with violence in her voice:

"Cruelty!" she said, "cruelty and oppression! Nothing is right that is based on that!"

"Are we looking for right and wrong?" I said. "Aren't we observing? Isn't that our reason for being here?"

"We are being changed ourselves," said Francoise, "by them, deliberately. At least—you are.'

Was that true? Was I being unduly influenced by the butterflies—beyond the point where I could observe, critically, in detail? I wanted another opinion, preferably Miss Hayes', but I felt reluctant to disturb her out of her great happiness. It was not as though she experienced this often, or was likely to. Indeed, happiness of this intensity is rare in adult humans, still more for those rather beyond middle life in whom the inevitable degenerative processes are already taking place, affecting the mind as they affect the tissues. Olga perhaps was the one to assist my own judgment. But I found it quite difficult to get her out of this pink and smiling state in which she sat, gazing at the immortal.

We three and the navigators walked some little distance away, out of the immediate area of acute happiness and across a rock ridge. I caught myself thinking of our geological specimens, all securely packed now for transit; I also thought how odd it was that our geologist had been so little affected by the butterflies, of the genetic and environmental differences in humans about which we still know so little. Our geologist hoped, for instance, that the Minerals Ministry people might be interested. I hoped not! We left Nadira, the youngest, and Miss Hayes, the eldest, to their contemplation and communion with ecstasy; I doubt if they noticed that we had gone. We sat down; one could see from here the windings of some of the major clefts and the plateau on which we had first seen the patterns of the caterpillars. What developed was a quite rational discussion. Were the butterflies morally entitled to behave with such cruelty to their own larval forms in order that occasional bliss among themselves should result? "If they could explain to the caterpillars—" said Olga, frowning.

"That's not possible," Francoise said, "I have tried myself—and they love me—to communicate to them that some day they will not just end, but will turn into butterflies. They cannot take it in. It is—completely out of focus. There is no way to transmit it."

"So that the whole thing seems like wanton oppression," Olga said heavily, thinking about it.

"It *is* wanton oppression!" Francoise said.

Olga went on as if she hadn't noticed: "That kind of thing has happened in human history, I think. When the good things of the present have been refused for the sake of the good things in the future. This postponement of enjoyment: yes, it happened both in the capitalist countries during their periods of major industrial development and in my own country after the revolution. But, even if it seemed like tyranny to many—for they would never themselves see the good things—there has always been the possibility of some communication, to some individuals. No, I know it's not the same, Francoise, but does the analogy help?"

Francoise shook her head. One of the navigators began to say that, on the whole, she agreed; she expressed it in mathematical symbols. Francoise paid no attention, only frowned. Then I picked it up, saying: "Isn't it more like what has been done in human history in the name of religion? When people were tortured and burnt alive in order to save their souls in another life, which most of them, perhaps, did not believe in. But the torturers did. Our ancestors did this in Europe, and I'm sure Nadira's did things fully as bad in Asia. So far, I have always found these actions inexplicable, and singularly revolting, but now I think I begin to understand them."

"Could we have stood by at the Spanish inquisition?" said Francoise.

"No, no! But then, the future state which was
125

postulated was in no sense *real*—"

"So you think—this—" she pointed back over the ridge, with her thumb "—is real—is justification for all that misery and pain? That frustration of all that made up for the caterpillars their—civilisation?'

"If you call it that, said Olga, and then: "Yes, perhaps you are right. Without the pattern-making, the wallowing, they are—nothing. Lumps."

For a moment I let myself slip back into communication with the butterfly. I said: "This that we have just seen, I believe it is justification.

"No!" said Francoise, "But no! These—individuals— are few—"

"But apparently undying. So the number increases," Olga observed.

"I ask myself," Francoise said, "if they are, truly, undying. Or if you merely believe the statement of the other butterflies because you want to."

I said: "I think we had better ask this one whether, in fact, it considers itself to be immortal, if so on what evidence. How long it has been in this state. Whether it can remember any less blissful state. Whether any others in its own state have died or—disappeared. There will be a lot to ask it—if we can." Olga nodded. I tucked my hand in under Francoise's arm: "Look, Francoise, whether we think all this is right or wrong, we can't alter it. We can't even try to alter it. We shall be leaving soon."

"Abandoning them," said Françoise, "those who need protection." She wiped the back of her hand across her eyes. "You are cruel!" she said, and pulled her hand away.

"Not really," said Olga, "it isn't our world. Is it?"

For a time Francoise sat there, pulled, we could see, between her love for the caterpillars and her knowledge that we were bound not to interfere in another world. It was against the most fundamental ethics of space exploration, and had been enforced on generations of humans by a whole series of mistakes, often based, like hers, on compassion. She knew all that, just as we did. We didn't have to rub it in. I began turning over in my mind the type of questions which we would need to ask the undying butterfly, and how they could be set into a single state of curiosity which could be transmitted. Olga was thinking the same thing, but knew less about the communication problem. She also wanted a botanical specimen from the butterfly's tree.

After a while Francoise began to talk quite reasonably, and to join in the discussion of what more must be found out. It seemed to me that the intensity of the communication with the undying butterfly of its own state was somewhat less. Perhaps it could now be disturbed. We went back. Miss Hayes turned her head and smiled at us.

Communication with this butterfly was much more difficult than through the ones with whom we had already developed it. We did not get any really satisfactory direct answers. We were none of us sure of the extent of the butterflies' memories. This one apparently remembered an earlier stage of development, clearly, however, as a butterfly only. It looked forward to further development, but we were completely baffled as to what this might be; perhaps there might even be intellectual states which were far beyond our own. Occasionally we got a hint of this, and I, at least, became fairly certain that the communicated happiness was only one part of the state in which the butterfly was; we could pick up the emotion but not the detailed intellectual state nor the whole of the aesthtic state.

There were certainly other butterflies developed in the same way, and becoming increasingly developed. No they did not end. They did not disappear. The predominantly red butterfly, which was trying to assist communication, kept on, also, communicating itself. We gathered that qualities might be developed in the "normal" butterfly by being with these others. Yet a time might come when they must go. It would want them to go. We asked as tactfully as we could if the red butterfly might become the same? It became desperately agitated and we sensed that it was possible but not likely. More probably, far more probably, because of something that had happened otherwhere, a doom would fall. The butterfly was terribly reluctant to communicate the fact that the caterpillar out of which it had developed, might have committed some action which would stop perfection—might, in fact, have become fertilised, in which case this butterfly too would, some day, perhaps suddenly, know that it must lay, and that the hated eggs would destroy it.

We realised, of course, that probably a simple cytological examination would make this clear. But the butterflies had always avoided physical contact with us, and we did not think it at all possible that we could even get blood samples. They avoided direct physical contact with the caterpillars, and it seemed as though their contact with the emergents was something demanding a tremendous effort.

Miss Hayes as well as myself had watched some of the hatchings. At least one in four appeared to be mutilated in some way, and was destroyed. She called us in and we managed to move one or two bodies into the camp before the wood crabs got them, and to make some anatomical and cytological observations. It appeared that there was a clustering of the cells which had undergone mitosis, so that, in time, something approaching a fertilised ovary might develop. But the anatomy was still rather uncertain, as though full differentiation had not yet taken place except in the external organs, the wings, legs and claws, eyes and so on. There seemed to be the beginnings of organs in the head region which we were uncertain about. Probably they had something to do with communication. There appeared to be a nervous connection with the antennae. If once we could get an adult butterfly in which complete development had taken place! There were a good many questions still to be answered about this world. These would be for future explorers. We had accumulated enough answers for a preliminary expedition. One must never do too much without taking time to think things over.

Meanwhile it was clear that the butterflies themselves considered that certain of their number were undying: and that the states in which they existed and would still further exist in the course of their development, were of such a kind as to justify anything which was done to make them attainable. In fact, there was never any sense, among the butterflies, that what was done to the caterpillars needed justification. It was an obvious process. As obvious, say, at the melting of ore to make steel or the grinding of wheat grains to make bread. We could not convey to them any sense of compassion, as humans know it, at any rate not to larval forms. It seemed to me that what they had shown to the laying and dying butterfly was a type of compassion, though not perhaps a human one. After all this, it was clear to me that we could not intervene on behalf of the caterpillars. At the end of a prolonged discussion I thought it was equally clear to Françoise and Nadira.

CHAPTER TEN

We had now definitely fixed our leaving date. Miss Hayes had been through all the calculations, checking in every detail with the navigators. She did it all with that meticulous care and complete confidence of hers which gave me, at least, such a sense of reassurance. Peder was the same, and so had Von Braun been in his time. None of the great leaders trusts to the unwavering accuracy of machines, everything was checked.

As always, there was a certain amount of discarding of material to decide on, as well as some deliberate committing to memory. We thought that we had, by now, all the information we were likely to get about this world, or at least the portion of it which we knew, and especially about the butterflies and caterpillars and their patterns of life; I was sure that this would be of major interest when we got back, and I was, on the whole, satisfied with the way we had handled it and my own solutions of the problems of communication. Further expeditions, after further thought and discussion about just these problems, might get communications a stage clearer; there were several of my colleagues whom I wanted to talk it all over with. I felt that it would particularly interest Vly. Again, a landing on some other part of this planet, or further exploration with some adequate means of transport, might disclose other patterns; we had very little idea of whether the butterflies were "everywhere". They seemed to assume that they were, but we could not be sure.

I noticed that Nadira was worried, and a little forgetful at a time when forgetfulness, ordinarily excusable, might have dangerous consequences. Francoise appeared to be acting with complete self-control, but at last Nadira told me that she was anxious. Francoise had been encouraging the young caterpillars to pattern-making activity; I knew that, and, though I deplored it, partly for their sake, since it might mean that they were destroyed as emergents, yet she was not really interfering in an active sense with the life of another planet. But Nadira said that she believed Francoise was also communicating with the butterflies, telling them that these special individuals, by whom they set so much store, did not live for ever. The only immortality was in egg-laying and the continuation of life through the larval form; she was in fact trying to undermine their confidence, in order that they should respect their larvae.

I was worried. This was definite interference. If the butterflies were right about the effects of the pattern-making and the wallowing, and if they were discouraged about their own life sufficiently to let the caterpillars alone to universal enjoyment of their patterns, then it was possible that a whole generation of malformed butterflies might emerge, crippled in the chrysalis, unable to be part of a butterfly life. Even if they were not blasted, could they survive? Would they not be victims for the wood crabs? Francoise refused to believe that pattern-making had definitely been proved to have anything to do with wing formation, and indeed, we only had the butterflies' word for it. She felt vehemently that the cruelty of the butterflies was as wanton as it seemed to the caterpillars. But I was inclined to believe that they knew what they were about.

However, I said to Nadira that I doubted if this attempt to influence them would have much effect on the butterflies. Was she sure that Francoise was really managing to communicate? It worried me that she had not spoken to me, as the senior expert, about this. Nadira said she thought the butterflies had understood. "And Françoise—she is so angry inside," Nadira went on, "I cannot reach her. She has gone past compassion into anger; that is so, I think. And anger is bad."

"Yes," I said, "anger makes one unsteady. And we can't have anything making us unsteady—even one of us—at the take-off."

I watched as carefully as I could, but I was myself very much occupied. Once, I remember, I woke early and saw Françoise still asleep, one of the caterpillars beside her; she had one hand stretched out lightly over it. I wondered whether I ought to try and pry into her mind, but, as you know, it is something one does with the greatest reluctance to a responsible adult. I wish now I had, all the same; I would have been justified in putting in a counter-interference, though this is normally so unethical. But after that I was immersed in the general problems. Even those who have been on twice as many explorations as I have been are quite worn out with the increased tensions, the rapid question and solution technique of both arrival and departure; these are wholly absorbing and somewhat exhausting after one comes to, with the problem temporarily solved.

At last we were away; the navigators were relaxing. We were proposing to go into time blackout quite soon. It was then, and already at a very great distance from our planet and its unanswered questions, that Françoise said, very steadily, to Miss Hayes: "That butterfly: the one that made you believe everything was right in their way of life—"

"The undying one," said Miss Hayes, and her mouth momentarily softened in memory.

"They are not undying," Françoise said. "Possibly they do not wear out, get no diseases and have no natural enemies. But they can be killed. I killed it."

This came through as a terrible shock to us all, for of course in that confined space there could be no privacy. I looked at Nadira and saw her face crumple into shock and sadness and tears fill up her eyes. Miss Hayes seemed to draw herself together, the smile fading off her mouth. "How?" she said.

"I took my weapon," Françoise said coldly.

"Only to be used for defence in the very last resort," Miss Hayes quoted from the code we all know by heart.

"I was defending them—and ourselves—from a lie," Francoise said.

"You know that you have committed—interference," Miss Hayes answered; we all waited, holding our breath; this was something I had never experienced before. The brown of Nadira's cheeks was beginning to be streaked with crying and slowly tears gathered also in Francoise's eyes. She knew what the penalty was. We all knew.

"It was necessary to tell you," Francoise said, "because this may alter the attitude of the butterflies; as it was meant to do. That was my only intention. And it must be reported to the next observers."

"Of whom you will not be one," Miss Hayes said.

Francoise whispered: "I know."

Nadira said, very pityingly: "Oh, Francoise, why did you not tell me? We might have thought—of some other way—"

"There was no other way," Francoise said.

Well, it was all quite straightforward. Such things do occur occasionally on expeditions. Some member, often one in whom empathy with the new kind of life is most strongly developed, interferes. The penalty, of course, is imprisonment for life on Terra. Beautiful, dull, safe old Terra. To be, as it were, wingless in the Galaxy. Prisoners of time. Francoise knew. She did not try to get out of it after the landing and the report. Very occasionally an explorer has made the attempt to get away with not telling, but this is so contrary to all modern ethical standards and behaviour patterns that it always throws those who have tried it into a state of mental block. What they have hidden

134

has then to be dug out of them, with all the resulting unpleasantness. Better to be like Francoise: to accept the crime and its punishment at the same time. And to reorientate oneself to some other way of living, as she is doing now. Probably she will decide to have a lot of children.

Yes, that was what she intended to do when we saw her last, Peder and I. But how will it work out? She had an explorer's psychological make-up and sympathies. Her curiosities have all been enlarged extra-terrestrially through deep-layer education. I cannot imagine that she will want to have fathers for her children who are anything but explorers, or possibly administrators. Even the Ministry men do some space travel. They will go off for years of her Terran time, spending most of it in blackout, but she will be ageing. When they come back she will be old and worn. She will have been worrying, as one does not worry on an expedition, when the whole of one's mental and psychological resources are necessarily directed in one way. This worry will show. There will be embarrassments and miseries. Francoise thinks still that she can face all that and deal with it, but will she be able?

And her children? She can never be the ageless, beautiful person—but was she really beautiful or is it just my memory?—that my own mother was. The days of taking personal photographs are over except among adolescents; she comes into a number of demonstration films, but there she is always working, not looking at one as I remember her looking and smiling. So how will Francoise seem? By the time her children are adolescents, she will be old. They will feel she is far off, in some impossibly distant group. She will have nothing to help them with. Nadira and Olga—even I, her senior and teacher—will still be reasonably young, able to do things and take in new ideas, but she will be old.

It will be difficult for us to talk to her.

An aged explorer has so much experience, has seen and

135

had to think about so much that he or she is as impressive as the great religious and political buildings of the Terran and Martian past, many angled, lovingly decorated, full of spaces for intense and special uses. Peder is like that; one can explore him endlessly, always learning something new. But Francoise can never have the experience which will make her old age into that kind of state; she will not have the extra time to get her experiences into order. For one can take consideration of data as well as pure meditation into time blackout and it will fall into order, will crystallise, will show its essential form, while the somatic frame of the considering mind is at complete rest, not age-ing. All this is something Francoise will never know.

I have taken her back into my communications research group for the moment, and everyone has been very welcoming, not showing blame, knowing that one punishment is enough. I just wonder how it will work out. When other members are away for five or ten of her years, taking turns, she will always be plodding along. She tells me that she thinks she will be able to avoid resentment of the rest of us. But for how long?

I can't believe that Francoise will ever make friends with the non-exploring Terrans. She will have the ordinary contact with them that we all have. There are plenty of common subjects, some quite pleasing and up to a point interesting. There is some research and technical work, and of course there are common amusements and games up to a point. But sooner or later one finds these light-weight common interests coming to an end; the non-explorers are pointed in another direction, are mostly interested in power anl pleasure which the rest of us cannot help considering to be of a rather worthless kind. Will there be anything deep for Francoise to share? Probably she will go on hallucinogen jags with some of them, but that usually ends by having unfortunate effects.

If she had the training and psychological make-up for it, she might have worked with the back-time explorers.

What they are doing can be most fascinating and genuine research work, whether on our own planet or others. But if she had been going to do that she would have had to make her choice much earlier. The best of them make it, and condition themselves for it from early childhood. Oddly enough, I have the idea that my girl, Lil-burn, T'o's child—and oh so pretty!—is quite possibly going to do that. Several of her age-group seem deeply interested, and have had a few preliminary back-time experiences. Sometimes I wonder if it has anything to do with her name. I wanted her to have one of those delicious polysyllabic African names, but T'o begged me to call her by one of the old names—the names of the Changers; like my own. I remember saying to him that there had been plenty of African changers, but he'd set his heart on one of the others and I couldn't bear not to let him have his way. So when, later, I told Lil about her name, she dug into the history and got an *apercu*, which made me think that this would perhaps be her territory. Just now she is working hard at Galactic history, not letting herself be deflected.

But it is too late for Francoise to make the personality modifications which she would have had to be making during her early years of education and play. Nor am I quite sure how the back-time groups would look at someone who had committed interference. They might think she was too much of a psychological risk. In back-time research one has to isolate oneself entirely from the scene observed, or so I understand.

No, Francoise made herself into an explorer and a communications expert, and it is within that framework that she must continue her life. There are, of course, still a few Terran species which appear to have intelligence, but with which we have not yet established communications. Francoise will be able to work on them. Oh yes, she is not quite cut off from the rest of us. But as the years go by we shall get more and more sorry for her, and I am afraid she will not care for that.

And sometimes I wonder whether her interference was really so much worse than the interference we all commit when we go to other worlds merely by being there, by standing and staring, by collecting information. When the early space travellers from other advanced worlds came first to Terra, we felt that we were being interfered with, simply because they were there, observing. We felt this so violently, if you remember, that we attempted to get rid of them, even with violence and always with great psychological disturbance. We have learnt better, of course, but only through experience. Non-interference as normally interpreted is a very coarse measure. We are always interfering, and it seems hard that this particular interference by Francoise should carry so heavy a penalty. I asked Miss Hayes what she thought. I remember she shook her head and asked me to think back quietly into that area of peace and joy beyond our experience or understanding which, because of human compassion and interference, was wiped out. And that is true. And if the penalty was not enforced where would we stop, we Terrans who in the course of history have so often not stopped in time? Perhaps in another dozen generations or so we shall get to the point where we feel it is wrong to commit even the interference of being in an alien world. Which would mean the end of space travel. Or would it? Could we perhaps become totally imperceptible? But we cannot see that far and it would be dull if we could.

Meanwhile, the interesting point is whether what Francoise did had any effect on the butterflies: whether it was such a blow to their beliefs, their pattern of life, that they made some kind of change in their behaviour: if so, whether this has lasted or has died out, the death of the immortal being in some manner explained away or made into something corresponding to poetry or music: whether it has resulted in more or less cruelty to the caterpillars: whether it will have any effect on the butterflies' reception of the next expedition of human beings: how far, in fact, the ripples spread. There must be another expedition, and some of us will have to be on it, probably as many as possible of the original personnel. I have a dreadful feeling that Francoise will come to the take-off point, join us in the final "tea-party" and try to see us off, behaving very bravely.

That, however, is still in the future. The first thing I asked after we landed was whether Pete was back. As soon as I heard this, I arranged to go straight over to the graft centre to hear the whole story, weigh up the evidence, and decide what to do next.

CHAPTER ELEVEN

Pete and the rest of his expedition gave us three days solid listening, viewing, as far as possible smelling, tasting and touching, assessing data, questioning, putting forward ideas for discussion. It was almost like an assimilation time, only far more packed, nothing apprehended quietly and easily, but all, as far as possible, short cut. Olga and Miss Hayes had both come with me and were most excited. For myself I found it of such intense interest that I didn't even recognise young Ket when he walked in!

It was a pleasure to see Daisy and Kali again, both in splendid condition, though a bit muddled by the time blackout. After all this lapse of Terran years, none of their animal friends were left, but they insisted that those who were there were the old ones. Kali's sister, Mani, had bred, and among her descendants was another extra bright young female jackal, whom Kali "knew" was her sister. They were very friendly to me and we went together to some of the films of the expedition. Daisy and Kali both recognised the world they had been in, trembled and growled in their throats with emotion. Daisy had a queer feeling about the grafts, perhaps in some way communicated by her grandmother; she knew they were important and somehow frightening and somehow wonderful; it was like the beginning of a mythology; I sensed it too, as she panted and whined to me. But the questions and discussions were too difficult for them, though I tried to interpret. Olga's sister, Rima, had a number of plants which Daisy and Kali smelt at with doubt and interest, dashing out afterwards to verify the old Terran plant smells.

I couldn't make out how their technician had got on. He did not express himself well, except perhaps to his animals. He had realised, of course, that his immediate environment would have disappeared when he got back, and he had wanted it to, especially one young woman. But he seemed no better at integrating into the new one. He spent most of his time with the jackals, and, although we tried to draw him into the discussions, he was not really interested. I suppose the truth is that unless one gets, as a quite young person, a deep realisation of the natives of time blackout; it can never be anything but a psychic shock.

The story, as Pete and the rest told it, appeared to be that this world from which the grafts had come was not in itself of great interest. The geology was undistinguished; it was badly lighted, being a long way from its sun, and perpetually damp. Certainly the grafts were there: almost everywhere in fact, apparently so much without consciousness that it was no wonder that the earlier expedition had treated them as not-life. A quick orbit of the planet, with long-distance visual recording, showed the same ecology everywhere. Yes, there was a good deal of dullish vegetation, thick, ungraceful, large-pored leaves, of a purplish colour for the most part: not attractive. Here Rima laughed and said Pete shouldn't apply Terran standards. Anyhow we must see her specimens and photographs. By the end of the expedition they had the plant physiology reasonably well taped; Olga asked a number of questions on this. A very large part of the planet was watery, though the water was mostly shallow, muddy and, to our senses, bad-smelling. Again Rima told Pete not to be Terran; there was nothing wrong with the water!

There were a number of fish-like and reptilian forms, though not quite like our own, as they were six-legged and had various other differences. All seemed to be egg-layers;

this had been noted by the earlier expedition which, however, for various reasons, had been rather casual over zoological observations. In fact, of course, it had been the usual business of having too many administrators on it; they had apparently thought there was something valuable, in their terms, on this planet. There wasn't, and it's really very silly and perverse of me to be pleased. Anyhow, Pete's expedition made plenty of observations. Some of the forms they found were so like our own early Terran dinosaurs that everyone began to talk of them as Diners. Their dining was continuous, as they had to take in a fantastic amount of the thick, purplish leaves to keep themselves going. Their brain area was small, and much of it was occupied by the problems of locomotion. Six large legs with flattened and partly webbed ends—they had no foot and toe structure like our own early reptiles, only a spreading of the bone end and ribs of cartilage—and quite complicated to work out. The expedition established an amiable but not very rewarding relationship with them, and were less successful in getting through to their cousins who lived entirely in the shallow water chewing away at the subaqueous vegetation which was much like that on land. The water reptiles had an overall hard skin, flexible enough but very tough and able to resist attacks by small leech-like forms which always hung on and sucked if the tough skin was abraded or cut.

But in the land reptiles the hard skin had broken up into scaly patches and areas of soft skin, especially around the legs and under the throat. And it was on these patches of soft skin, almost always on female Diners, that the expedition found the grafts, apparently living as straightforward parasites. It took some time to find out what was actually happening. Even so there were possibilities of variant interpretations of the life cycle which we discussed during the three days.

It seemed that the grafts, which grew to about the same size as the Terran ones, were not much inconvenience to the large Diners, but could have been easily rubbed off if they had so wanted. But they did not want. At least the females did not want. Pete was quite certain of that. Nor was it ordinary parasitism. As with us and the experimental animals, there was a true graft relationship; they became part of their hosts, though, without committing interference, it was impossible to find out how completely similar their cell-structure and biochemistry was. It was quite definite that the female hosts enjoyed having them. The communication man on the expedition—and I found myself getting a bit jealous of him!—was certain of this, and his evidence seemed to me quite positive. The great beasts became maternal towards them as, being reptiles not mammals, they could not be to their own children. Their long necks arched down towards them in a caress. Their forked tongues darted in and out gently over the grafts, whose external texture was obviously pleasing to them, as was their stiffening.

So far so good. It now appeared that at certain times, roughly every three or four months, possibly governed by climatic conditions, but a series of graphs threw no real light on this, these females went down into the shallow water. They rolled about there and laid a great number of small eggs which, as they came out, were rather casually fertilised by the males who came down into the water with them, probably attracted by some smell or a similar simple stimulus. At other times, though they drank copiously, they did not actually go right into the waters. When this egg-laying took place the grafts disappeared; it looked, from all the observations, as though they deliquesced just as Ariel and the rest had done.

What triggered this off? Was it only the water, or was it something to do with the egg-laying and fertilisation? Was there, for example, some kind of hormone at work? To answer this question would have meant a great deal of laboratory work, and action which would not have been compatible with non-interference. It is quite possible that the simplest hypothesis, that it was merely the water, was the true one.

The next stage was a little obscure. But it had something to do with the eggs. It seemed as though there was some meeting up between some of the eggs and the deliquesced grafts. It could not be put into the simple form of a union between the eggs and cells or groups of cells from the graft, since the cell walls had disintegrated. But after all a cell is something of very great complexity, as we first began to realise in the mid-twentieth century. Pete's micro-observations were not altogether clear, partly perhaps because at these times the male Diners were particularly irritable. Some of the expedition had been kicked or head-swiped into the water themselves while trying to get samples. There was a very funny bit of film which Hima had taken.

At any rate, the end result was that only a few of the eggs survived, and became little lizard-like, darting Diners, rather attractive I thought them. The others were in some way absorbed and grew into small grafts, ten or twenty centimetres long, rather like the small ones we had brought up without hosts in the laboratory. These oozed about among the vegetation, putting out pseudopodia and ingesting leaves which had been partly chewed up by the Diners during their endless untidy eating. Now and then a Diner would accidentally bite one; this always had the same effect. The Diner would swing its head violently, curling its lip, and bits of the bitten-up graft would be flung about. Some of these bits would land on the unscaly patches round the tops of the Diner's legs, and almost always, in some way that was so far not clear, would manage to stick on and then work their way through the skin and symbiose. It seemed, in fact, as though the skin softened to admit them.

Then came another interesting point. If the accidentally chosen host was a male, the graft did not arouse "maternal" feelings, was looked on as a nuisance (again the com-

145

munication expert was definite) and was, sooner or later, rubbed off. Occasionally it held on, but never seemed to grow to full size. Sometimes those which had been rubbed off died, but sometimes they would get another chance and be snapped into by a female. If they died they deliquesced rapidly.

All this to some extent benefited the Diners, since if all their fertilised eggs had been able to hatch into little Diners, the whole planet would have been eaten flat; there would have been far too many, and there were no very efficient predators. There were other possible benefits. What value can one attach to the kind of enjoyment the female Diners got out of their grafts? That is more questionable, though I think one must attach some value to it. They seemed also to grieve at their loss when, at the time of fertilisation, the grafts dropped off, or at any rate they got a sense that all was not well; but this grief was not nearly so strong as their enjoyment before. How it could all have evolved was very difficult indeed to understand.

But it did throw a good deal of light on what had happened to us and our grafts. We were mammals, and that had altered the cycle. But it showed that the females among us behaved in certain ways like the female Diners. It also explained the curious urge which some of us had towards water. It also tentatively suggested that if, as a general rule, the grafts were left on the Terran host or apart from the host for much longer than their normal life cycle they disintegrated and, as individuals, died as they would have in their home planet. Nor had they any chance of continuing as they did before. Sometimes this disintegration could be put off for a time as it occasionally had been with the animal grafts, but it was quite uncertain why or when this would happen. It might well have been something to do with the change in diet when they were grafted on to carnivores. Again it was possible that when they were re-grown, as ours had been in laboratory conditions, from excised pseudopodia, it might count as a new life.

Pete thought, but couldn't be sure, that the graft attach-ment only began to narrow into the typical neck that there had been between me and Ariel, for instance, immediately before disintegration, happening very quickly, not slowly as with us. This was only one of the loose ends. There were others. But obviously further research was necessary.

It was clear why the original expedition which had brought the first grafts or pieces of graft back with them supposed they were dealing with something well below the level of consciousness. If the grafts partook of the nature of their mother Diners, they were just not bright. The grafts could not go one better than their hosts. But what would happen if a graft which had been part of an in-telligent being was taken back to the home world? Perhaps only interference and unhappiness.

One of the first things we decided was that we must try some large reptilian, or at any rate egg-laying, hosts, dif-ficult as it might be to explain to them just what was hap-pening. We thought of the great turtles or the large Komodo lizards. Not very bright either! We thought of crocodiles or alligators, but large crocodiles are singularly unaccommodating, however carefully one tries to condi-tion them; as laboratory animals their genes are just not suitable. But at least we would know if something near the normal life cycle could be repeated in Terran conditions, and we might find out whether the stimulus for disintegra-tion was simply the presence of water or somtething else in the maternal bloodstream. It might be that some reptilian eggs might respond to the deliquesced grafts and re-grow individuals. "What about batrachians?" someone asked. It was clear that there were no Terran frogs or toads large enough to take grafts, but the freshly fertilised eggs might be mixed into the water at the critical moment. Then one of the Martians suggested one of their own egg-laying aquatic types. It had never been imported on to Terra, but we knew more or less what it was: something of a pest in the canals, and we would have to be careful not to let any

147

loose on our own planet or the Police crowd would be a
ter us. On film it looked very like a larger version of t'
common toad, a real old Bufo.

I said to Pete: "You got some fresh graft tissue, didr
you?"

"Yes," he said, "at the various stages."

It occurred to me as he was talking that he was an a
tractive bit of goods with bright, wild hair, a crinkle rou'
his eyes, and a good smile. But somehow it didn't set '
the old tingle. The funny thing was that I didn't think at '
about Ket. I kept thinking about Peder whom I'd spok'
to long distance but had not seen yet. Was I getti'
monandrous? Surely I wasn't that aged! I found myse'
rather upset and shocked, then thought no, it was just ev
so simply that Peder was more interesting than all the re
put together. And if only he would agree to it we wou'
have another baby, a daughter, a corn-silk-hair'
daughter. But that wasn't what I was here to think about

"Well," I said, "I think we've got to repeat the exper
ment. After all the grafts were all material which had go'
through a number of artificial cycles, or rather not go'
through them. It was as if they'd been cast off and th'
snapped up again and re-grown and cast off a dozen time
maybe more. Right?" He nodded. "The whole thing m'
be different now, possibly stronger," I said. "I'll take
fresh graft."

We talked it over. Pete agreed. Olga and Miss Hay
worried about it more than I did. There was one tricky b'
It seemed as though the grafts always attempted, as
were, to persuade their hosts not only into maternal lo'
but into the act of bathing, of going deep into the wate
Might they not also tempt them to the act of fertilisatio'
How would this be with a Terran host, or rather, hostess'

"I don't think so," I said. "I remember that with po'
Ariel, my normal menstrual cycle stopped. It was
though I had already been fertilised."

"Yes, but with the new material—" said Pet'

148

"—knowing what we do know, it might hold up human ovulation, then restart it, then get you to bathe. Supposing the deliquesced graft managed to make an entry while you were in the water? That might be exceedingly awkward, mightn't it? One doesn't know what the uterine reaction might be."

I agreed that this was something one would have to be very careful about. But one could easily immerse the graft without immersing the relevant parts of one's own body. The same could be done, with a bit of care, for all the mammals.

"As to ordinary fertilisation," said Pete, "here's my young Ket still mooning about—"

"Come, come, Pete," I said, "I'm not interfering in his age group."

"You think not, Mary?" said Pete. "You have. We can't get you out of his head. He keeps on talking about you. He thinks of me as old dad! How long is it in his years since you left for your butterflies?"

"Oh dear," I said, "I didn't think it had gone that far. What does he admire about me, Pete?"

"A lot of nonsense," said Pete, and he was rather cross, understandably I thought, "self-possession; confidence; knowledge and know-how. Moral courage, he says! All the things he hasn't got yet himself."

"It wouldn't be natural at his age," I said. "But he'll get them all right later on. Bound to with his heredity. Still, I'll see what I can do. I suppose the one he's really after is his mother. Silis is all that. And as there's a barrier, I'm the next best."

"You're half Silis's age, Mary," said Pete, "and a lot more attractive—

But I wasn't having any. At the moment it bored me whether with Ket or his father. I was only anxious to get on as soon as possible with the new grafting experiments.

CHAPTER TWELVE

I had to see Peder first, so I rushed back. It is still wild in the mountains, still full of echoes and silence; I slowed down after Trondhjem. It is so good to change travel pace, it is almost a time change. He came to meet me. So did Jon and Viola. Suddenly I felt a shedding of some residual blame that had stayed with me from the butterflies, and also, of course, from having been deputy leader on an expedition where someone committed interference. In fact, neither Miss Hayes nor I had been blamed for this, but one cannot help it when an event begins to set up rings of consequences.

Jon had been a small boy when I left, well integrated into his group, with a good all-round intelligence. He was almost full grown now, long-legged with a fair skin that burned red. Peder must have been just like that, rather shyly affectionate, showing off all the skill and courage that are natural at that age. I kept looking from one to the other; Peder himself had aged, but not as much as I had thought he might, since he hadn't been able to keep out of one amusing little expedition which had cleared up a few points, and had given him a couple of years of time blackout. It was a non-life world with some interesting pseudo-magnetic echo effects which his mathematical sensitivity had finally elucidated, but luckily there was nothing to interest Minerals! All the time we were talking about it I was looking for signs of age, but could only think that his blue eyes had deepened in his head, and his hair had a more brightly silver wave to it.

But it did seem to me that Viola was having difficulties, and that these were my responsibility in so far as they were my recessive genes exposed by not having another parental chromosome coming out in her. She had been growing up happily in her own group, playing the intellectual snap-on television games that were so popular with them. But now, inevitably with my genes, she wanted to explore, and there were difficulties. On the mere matter of size she could not use the standard equipment. Not everybody would be willing to redesign and remake what she would have to handle. Space travel is obviously the most expensive thing we do, though, of course, the most worthwhile. But sometimes we on our side have to argue with the administrators; she would have to convince people that she was specially worthwhile, and I would have to help her. By now I had a sufficiently good reputation as an expert for any child of mine, especially perhaps an unfathered one, to be taken seriously.

It is odd, nowadays, for a parent to have so much responsibility towards a child. If anything, it is likely to be the other way. One does not yearn tenderly, owningly, over ones children, not at least after the first few months. One treats them as human beings, individuals, with the inalienable right not to be owned, to have their own space and their own time. Even the earth-bound, the non-explorers, realise this, disassociating children and guilt. Yet I could not now rid myself of this curious sense of blame. Several times I returned in dreams to the butterflies and more than once to the Epsies and Rounds, though in this dream Peder usually managed to explain it away. Once I dreamed back to the space voyage with Vly. In my dream I made the other decision: to terminate the pregnancy. But I woke with a sense of horror and immensely increased blame. This was no way out of the situation.

Whatever genes had determined me to communications had also determined Viola. She knew her theory backwards. She had practised on various Terran species. I watched her getting in touch with an arctic fox, being allowed to come near, establishing confidence. It was well done. But unhappily the genes had determined other things. Apart from the headaches, which were better, one or two small allergies I have were much worse with her. A normal allergy is fairly easy to deal with; hers were more difficult. And again she was much attracted to men. This was all very well in the television games which were great courts of flirtation with their own codes. But the men who liked her brilliant image were sometimes less pleased to meet her in the three feet of flesh and blood which the intellect inhabited, even with the exquisitely delicate skin and hair that was half the normal thickness, impossibly silky, so that shining it floated in an entirely elfin way—oh I let myself think crazily and with deep love up there on the snowfield!

We are better than we used to be at respecting and getting on with unaccustomed forms of life. It was not as though my Viola were in any way deformed mentally or physically. But she could not take over the controls, say, of an ordinary machine, so that she was out of a good many pastimes of her age group. Men tended to be kind to her and that sort of kindness is almost the opposite of the sort of thing she wanted. But she was a beautiful skier, which meant that she and Peder saw a lot of one another easily and without his appearing to be too inquisitive or over-anxious about her life. She did not talk to me at once, but suddenly late one evening when we had been talking about cybernetics she burst into tears. For a time I could not tell how much this was because of her difficulties in becoming an explorer and how much was because a particular young man hadn't gone as far as she'd wanted. I wasn't used to being in this sort of relation with someone not in my own age group, and I didn't feel I should in any professional sense pry into Viola's mind.

However, I had to make some sensible suggestion, and I

aked her if she would like to go to Mars for a conference with Peder; she could go up country. Vly would fix it. This would mean experiencing a modified time blackout and getting the first feeling of space. I remembered saying to her, "If you can get anywhere with znydgi youll be cleverer than any of us." I talked to her a bit about time blackout as well, remembering how it had seemed when my mother talked to me.

There was snow after that, and all of us skiing and the bright glare of the sun making sharp angles and thin planes of dazzle, the same sun for all of our planets, for our Martian fellow explorers and the throbbing brains and wet crawlers of Venus, for the colonists on Saturn and Jupiter—and a tiny spark of light far in the sky for others. I caught up too on all the news: the rather boring administration news with the Health crowd looking out for bacteria mutations or possible invaders from other worlds, and the Defence crowd getting into their temporary nightmares about some other galaxy and the Police crowd reporting lapses and atavisms: occasional colonial difficulties and all that. How various research projects were going on Terra and elsewhere. What was happening in the arts—here one was most closely in touch with some of the non-explorers, the time-bound, getting in their bits of eternity not from time blackout but from the arcing of beauty, and also with one's own young, who perhaps take the arts more seriously than we explorers do. And gossip, of course, who was where after what, who was having a baby, and so on. Peder told me the 513 had gone off on a small and particularly dangerous expedition, of which all trace had been lost. Even though she had not actually been blamed or accused of allowing interference on the Minerals Expedition, the thought of what had happened had become more and more a burden to her.

I felt a share of that; I might have guessed sooner. If I had not obstinately set myself on the wrong track! Peder too felt that he should have guessed. And yet it was that expedition which had brought us here, and which was responsible for young Jon.

And then it was time to get back into work time and think about the grafts. But Viola seemed pleased about her expedition to Mars; Peder was arranging it. I was pleased too; there had been a time when I had felt that Viola was almost bound to find her destiny among non-explorers, but I couldn't be sure yet how it would work out so I didn't say too much. I asked her to take Vly some Terran seeds; the geneticists had been altering some plants for him. They would probably all be going to heighten the tone of one of his wines and make it still more delicious. Or should I say "hers"? Peder had a message for me from Vly that he had gone female and had a child. It made me feel most peculiar, so rooted we are still in our Terran conventions. However this, like the earlier accident, would be only a temporary deviation from normal bisexuality. I wondered what had thrown him into it.

Meanwhile a message from the centre had been flashed through the bases to Mars, and they had sent off some of their pseudo-toads practically at once. They were now installed, in the best approximation we could make to home conditions; they were not very attractive, for they did not have the beautiful eyes of our own Terran toads. In fact, it was doubtful how much they could see. But they did lay eggs in water, which were fertilised as they came out, and their diet was partly at least vegetarian, though they seemed not averse to trying anything; they stood about two feet high at the shoulder and were very broad; you could see how a few of them would block a canal! Their skin was tougher than that of our own toads, slightly scaly, but there were soft areas where they could take grafts. We stood round, looking at them; if one dropped a small object of any kind on to their skin, they could twitch it off to quite a distance. I thought they smelt dreadful, and so did Daisy.

She and Kali were both in a state of great excitement

and longing to bounce all over me, communicating by voice and tongue. I always found it faintly unpleasant to be licked by the jackals; most of the dogs had been trained to take other proteins, but the jackals were still carnivores, and had to have the dead bodies of other animals provided for them. Occasionally a devoted technician would ask that his body on death might be given to his animals, but this was useless unless owing to old age or retiral he had been away from them for a long time. Otherwise they would recognise his body and refuse to touch it in an act of violence. But meat-eating did make the jackals less pleasant to talk to than the dogs, though they were just as intelligent and perhaps rather more original-minded. The hyaena was intelligent too, and could be communicated with; leopards tended to be perpetually otherwhere.

They had all been introduced to the grafts they were going to have, and were thrilled at the prospect. It had been explained that this was new and important. One male jackal whom I had never taken to though he was bright enough, was going to be used as the control. The znydgi bounced about, whisking their pretty forked tails and wriggling their long iridescent eyebrows, facing into the sun and making their piping whistling noise which, although one could imitate it perfectly, seemed never to communicate. I always found them irritating for this reason, though some people seemed to be able to watch them continually. Sometimes they stopped playing and lay still, pretending to be striped stones, as they might well have been on Mars, if at least that was what they were doing! It seemed so very peculiar to have failed altogether to get through to them. Daisy felt the same. She was full of curiosity, and had many friends of other species, though her main affections were centred on humans. I remember she smelt me all over and began asking some of these cheerful but rather embarrassing canine questions, first about T'o, whom she remembered, and then, finding she was out of date, about Peder and me. I pulled her ears and tickled all her favourite bits. Kali liked to have different bits tickled.

At the same time I worked with the animal technicians, trying to explain to the other species what was happening. I found the sows curiously uninterested. But there was a young cow, Trude, who seemed able to get at what was to be done. But she could not, I noticed, be communicated with except at certain times. When she was chewing the cud she went into a condition of near trance; it was apparently a period of happiness and vague visualisation or olfactualisation, but the intellect and the sense of communication cut out altogether.

Olga had stayed on for a bit with her sister; they had persuaded a good many of her plants to grow, especially the thick-leaved, dominant variety. Olga's plant chemistry was becoming more and more sensitive, she seemed to know what a plant wanted from traces of evidence which were not apparent to the rest of us. She and Rima were constantly getting into long and maddeningly technical colloquies. I tried to get her to take a graft, but she was very definite that she was not going to; in fact I think she found the whole idea rather shocking and unpleasant, though she was very loyal to me about it.

We all had our grafts at the same time. So did a Martian volunteer, Zloin. I had mine again on the thigh, Zloin on the soft tissue close to the shell. We had decided that we should get on to reasonably intimate terms if possible, so as to be able to compare symptoms in depth, and I got Zloin (this, of course, is only an approximation) to vocalise his name—or rather hers, since he was thrown into female monosexuality soon after taking the graft, and remained so during the course of the experiment. We decided that it was important that we all, Martians, humans, dogs, jackals and other species, should exchange as much information as possible, especially if we had previously had grafts and if the present experience was at all different. Various samples were to be taken regularly and tests made: possibly uncomfortable, though not painful. This was all very well, but we had not reckoned with the fact that the grafts would affect us in such a way that we would be highly suspicious of all tests and, as regard the grafts themselves, we would want to huddle over them secretly instead of speaking about them or even experimenting on them, openly. In a way Daisy expressed what we all felt, getting across her thought that the graft was really inside her. All we saw was pretend.

Zloin hadn't had a graft before. The other Martians who had done it did not at all want to try again. In any case, both of them were going on other expeditions. I think they tried to dissuade Zloin, but on Mars, as here, there are, fortunately, plenty of individuals who are not to be dissuaded from experimenting.

CHAPTEH THIRTEEN

Certainly there were differences, but these seemed to have to do with the vitality of the fresh grafts. We had tried both the surgical grafting technique which we had originally used, and also the mere laying on of the graft on the skin of the host with a very light bandage to hold it temporarily in place. I persuaded Daisy that this was a more interesting and praiseworthy thing to do, and that I would do it myself; it worked with both of us, also with some of the Martian pseudo-toads, but not with any heavy skinned animals such as the sows, mares and cows. Zlion had preferred the other method.

The grafts grew a good deal faster, and had a more pronounced effect. Disconcertingly soon Zloin was in full female monosexuality, and I was in the state of fuss and malaise that I had been in at a much later stage with Ariel. The sexual cycle stopped in all the animals as well as in myself. We all took in what it was thought could be passed on. My own idea was that it would be interesting if Daisy and I listened to the same kind of music to see if it would pass to our grafts; I found she was very partial to woodwind—in fact I found out a lot about canine aesthetic tastes. It was curious how working together led us into quite a different phase of relationship. In fact it has ended with Daisy deciding to retire from the centre and transfer her affection to Peder and me.

Then after a relatively short time we all began to pine for water, in spite of the fact that there were ample washing facilities and an abundance of cool drinks and fruit. It was much more definite this time, and I gradually became obsessed with the idea that for the sake of my graft I must somehow swim. I would be able to shake this off when discussing it coolly with Pete or Olga or any of the rest, but when I was alone or communicating with any of the other hosts the compulsion would come back in an apparently more and more objective way. Olga was very worried and told me I should get rid of the graft before it started owning me; I found myself pretending to agree, but cleverly making difficulties. And all the time I realised that I was enjoying my unscientific and delinquent deception, just as I was enjoying baiting and frustrating Olga. But in what sense was I me?

Ordinarily I would have communicated with Zloin through the usual tactile channels, but now that she had the graft she did not want to have her sexual organ touched, however gently. One does not in the ordinary course of an expedition or a joint experiment meet many Martians who are due to give birth, and I had not realised that this was normal pre-parturition Martian behaviour. I only supposed it was due to some communication blunder by myself and decided that it could only be put right by the sharing of a bath. How I came to this conclusion I cannot now see; but at the time it appeared to be common sense. I believe my rationalisation was to the effect that close communication could take place through the medium of water; this is just not so. But all my thought processes were bent by this obsession.

Pete told me afterwards that I became very odd to talk to; he took some photographs without my noticing and I can barely recognise myself; it is as though I had been trying to hide. One useful effect it had was that Ket was completely put off. He came to see me, and apparently I tried to get him to be my ally on this matter of bathing. In fact I remember doing so and congratulating myself on my own cleverness and oblique approach. However, he was scared and went dashing off back to his own age group. It seemed to me, not only that the whole point of the experiment lay in the crucial bath, but also, though I knew in a way that the idea was being forced upon me, that one was being infinitely cruel to the innocent and loved graft if one did not accede to what it needed.

This time I kept the name of my graft to myself. So I noticed did Zloin, though each of us had communicated to the other as a secret that our grafts were named. All the animals kept licking at their grafts. I wondered what effect this would have, but obviously there was not enough watery stimulus to do anything drastic. I fondled mine, and Zloin fondled hers, each of us tending to get into a corner.

As the days went by, our conduct became increasingly abnormal and indeed in a sense delinquent. I found that my graft (and still after all these years I don't like even to remember its name!) was already responding to the music which it—or I—had been hearing, by regular rhythmic movement of body and pseudopodia, which I found curiously gratifying. I responded by kissing and even licking and gently biting my graft, just as the Diners had done. Then it would wriggle or ripple all over, pressing against me. These wriggles seemed to penetrate me and, where I had found Ariel's incursions between my lips rather disquieting, this one's were welcome. And yet now, I cannot equate the taste of my graft's exploring pseudopodia tips with any range of tastes that I know. I can only remember the feeling of hidden, but complete satisfaction that they set up in me. The same seems to have been true for all the hosts. I ought, of course, to have reported all this, and also to have found out whether Daisy's graft, who had heard the same music as mine, also responded. I did not do so. It was part of my secret. In fact, I was becoming anti-scientific. Luckily Nadira, who had come over to see how things were going, noticed that Daisy's graft was moving in just the same rhythmic way. She wanted to talk to me about it, but when she came to see me I pretended to be asleep.

We had decided at the beginning that we would let certain of the host animals into a pool of water and see what happened. The intention was to let the Martian pseudo-toads be the first, and the pool was there just by their house. It had even a certain architectural elegance, and I kept on thinking about it. Olga had induced some of the graft-world aquatic plants to grow there. We had grafted on to several female toads, apparently to their pleasure, but the males shrugged off the grafts with a determined twitch or two. We thought it quite possible that there might be a complete recapitulation of the dinosaur cycle with the grafts breaking up and attaching themselves to the toad eggs. In fact, I had been the one who discussed the implication of this most thoroughly in the beginning. But now in the most peculiar way I began to feel jealous of the pseudo-toads. Why should their grafts be fulfilled and not mine? In one of my moments of sanity, or return to my normal self, I said this—laughingly even—to Pete. "But Mary," he said, "if the cycle recapitulates the grafts disappear completely—that's the end of them. Do you just mean you want your graft to disappear?"

"Oh no," I said. "Oh no. You don't understand." And my hand lay caressingly on my graft.

"Well of course if some bit of them latches on to an egg, it's not the genetic end—" How little he knows, I thought, of what kind this fulfilment is! Yet I could not have put into words what I felt myself to know. I had regressed into a pre-intellectual state.

Then one afternoon when I was lying in a sort of warm haze of longing and scheming, in which plans and possibilities merged into one another, I began to hear a violent din. After a while I realised that Zloin had reached out with her toes and was communicating a question.

eluctantly I replied that it was Kali and Mani. But there
as more to it than that. In a little Pete Lorim came in,
oking terribly upset, and with one arm bandaged. I felt
if I didn't want to hear, but he made me listen, and then
aited while I communicated with Zloin, making sure that
e too had taken it in. Apparently both jackals had been
ken with the symptoms of coming on heat and had
arted yelping. This had set off some of the other car-
vores, including even poor dear Daisy who is always so
hamed of herself when she finds herself making emo-
onal noises instead of communicating sensibly with those
e loves. Their technician, the one who had been on the
ace journey, who had always got on best with the
ckals, and had never for a moment had any fear of them,
ent along to see if he could quieten them. But when he
ent into their play yard they both sprang at his throat,
ocked him over and bit him savagely, then raced out.
hey did not, apparently, look for the dog jackal, but he
as in another part of the centre, where they probably
uld not smell him. As the poor technician staggered up,
eeding and screaming, Pete and a couple of others tried
 intercept the jackals, who in the ordinary way had
und the grafts stopped them from any quick movement.
Not now. With the grafts streaming out behind them
ey galloped to the toad's pool and plunged in, after tear-
g open Pete's forearm. "And then?" I asked, trembling.

"The grafts melted off them," said Pete ."Just like they
d with the Diners. And have probably got inside the
ckals."

"Yes," I said and shut my eyes. "Yes." But all the
me, with another part of myself, with what was left of
y intelligence, I realised how dangerous all this was, how
e graft had effected a complete character change on the
ckals, as my graft was doing on me—and as I wanted it
.

"I'd get you to talk to the jackals," said Pete,

"but—Mary, I don't trust you. I don't trust you, see!" We
well, I thought, perhaps she's right about that.

What Pete did, sensibly enough, was to get hold
Francoise. She'd been my pupil, and she was very hap
to be asked, to be counted as one of us again. I did
know this till afterwards, but she managed to get throu
to the jackals. They were terribly upset and miserab
Kali especially; she was devoted to her technician, an
could not even remember what she had done. Whe
Francoise made her lick his blood, which was on her pa
and lips, she howled and howled in misery and gui
Luckily the jackals had not killed their technician, thoug
they had been near doing it;; his right hand had been bad
crushed.

Meanwhile the dogs, especially Daisy, turned a real ba
rage of hate and blame on to them. What they had do
was temporarily to ruin the whole relation betwee
animals and technicians, something which was of gre
value on both sides. And then the pseudo-toads bega
They had been left free to move into the pool and mov
they did; the males clasped the females and fertilised th
emerging eggs, the grafts melted away into the water an
now it was possible to make a whole series of biochemic
and cytological observations of great interest. These we
the basis, of course, of Pete Lorim's prize work. I remen
ber with astonishment that he asked me to come along an
look, but I shook my head. In some way, I didn't kno
how, my own graft was not ready. Or I was not read
Something was on the verge of happening that could n
be hurried. And I suppose I realised that, if I saw an
allowed what I had seen to influence me, I might hav
been thrown back into a normal frame of mind.

Then Trude's turn came. She jumped the fence that
mild young heifer wouldn't ordinarily have looked at an
got at the pool, which by now was heaving with th
pseudo-toad eggs. Again two or three people tried to sto

er; she put her head down and charged, knocking Olga
ead over heels. She got in and rolled about, and her graft
eliquesced. It was then that Pete, without telling me, sent
or Peder.

What happened to the jackals and to Trude was that the
rafts entered and made contact with the eggs, including
hose in the ovarian follicules. This made itself apparent a
ew days later in violent pain. Mani went into fits and
ied. Kali and Trude were operated on and the ovaries
emoved.

But with Daisy things went rather differently. She told
ne about it afterwards when we were all sane again, my
oor lovely, silk-coated, golden Daisy! In a way it was all
uite simple; there was a dog mastiff wandering about. He
vas a great ally of Pete, a quiet dignified dog, and sud-
lenly his smell, which she had barely noticed before,
ecame overpowering. "I wanted, I wanted," whimpered
Daisy while I stroked her.

"I know, Daisy," I said. "I wanted too."

So when Daisy got to the water her graft had already
rapped her into fertilisation. She was the last one of the
mammals to get to the pond. It was quite plain that the
ame thing was happening to them all, and pointless to let
t go on. But the technicians and research workers had
een so unused to putting any real physical restraint on the
nimals in their charge that everything had to be im-
rovised. They started getting ready some syringes with
ariously graded doses of hypnotics. Francoise proved
erself extremely useful, calming down and checking and,
'm afraid, lying to these frantic females of various spe-
ies. It was very fortunate that the female hyaena was not
ne of the first to be influenced. If she had been she would
robably have killed her technician. Only the znydgi were
completely quiet and unworried. Their grafts had in all
ases remained quite small, and oddly inactive considering
how playful their hosts were.

But that was something I got to know afterwards. While it was going on I heard the noise but paid little attention. Nor did Zloin, who was occupying herself with the kind of mathematical puzzles that for some reason give Martians pleasing and restful surface sensations. I remember how Vly used to do them at difficult moments in the space voyage. A Martian in normal bisexuality ordinarily does two at once, but Zloin toyed with one at a time slowly. She was withdrawn as I was, waiting. I found movement difficult, and yet I knew when the time came I would get strength. Then with a rush it all happened. My recollection immediately afterwards was so displeasing that I have almost blotted it out. What I am fairly certain of is that I was completely under the influence of the graft, except that far down, almost smothered, there was still a very small quietly struggling observer. I remember that Peder came, and that this either coincided with, or was the stimulus towards, the fertilisation which the graft was demanding. "You made no bones about it," said Peder afterwards. "But I had the case history. I wasn't going to fertilise you for that, my love. But if Pete hadn't given me the histories—!"

And then I was struggling desperately towards the water, and my tiny inside observer was considering that the original plan of bathing part of the body without allowing any possibility of entry by the deliquesced graft was highly unpractical. I was battering at Peder and Pete, Olga and Francoise, and the terrible thing was, I was winning. We can't any longer put our full hearts into violent restraint of another human being. Whereas I had ceased to be a civilised scientist. I bit Francoise, my pupil. I hit Pete a crack on his bitten and inflamed arm and he let me go. Only Peder was still holding me, and I was stronger than he was, younger and stronger, and the water was so near and I could smell and almost feel it!

Then Olga cut the neck of the graft, cut into it, into me—

She did it with a scalpel, very skilfully. But the neck had not dwindled down as the neck between Ariel and me had done. I—or it—bled and bled. They were dabbing on dressings and bandaging and holding on and trying to get through to me. I was aware of utter disaster, utter grief, but could not place it. Then someone dug into me with a hypodermic, and I floated off into night and nothing.

CHAPTER FOURTEEN

I woke in a room I didn't know, crying. Tears ran into my ears, tickling and wet. What was it all about? I sank once more.

Zloin was in the same room on the bed next to me. How? Strange, unreadable. Without her graft. Francoise was shaking me, saying: "Speak to her. Get through! I can't." After a long time I stretched out my hand, felt for her fingers, then rolled over so as to touch the other hand as well. Sadness came at me, loss, disturbance, reentment against Terrans. "Zloin," I vocalised. There was a chip off the edge of her shell, close to where the graft had been; there was an area of bruising. I noticed that first. Then I noticed something else. I had by now had considerable experience of Martians, and it seemed to me that Zloin was swinging between male and female.

I forced myself to sit up, dizzily, then to stand, Francoise at one elbow, Peder at the other. Where had he come from? I looked down at my thigh. It was still bandaged, still painful in a muffled way. I went across to Zloin, lay close, and began on deep tactile communication to and from all sensitive areas. Suddenly the barriers went. Zloin started communicating.

Considering Martian physiological make-up and the occlusive nature of the shell, Zlion had been in less dange than I. But nobody was quite sure what might be going t happen, and the Terrans felt an extra responsibili: towards her. So it had been decided to remove the graft.

169

The neck of hers had constricted slightly more than mine, but even so there was profuse bleeding. Pete had tried very hard to keep both grafts alive, but had failed to do so. They stayed no more living than a severed leg. At the last moment he had decided to try and regraft one of them, mine. Francoise had offered herself. They gave her as large a dose of stock antigens as she could take with even moderate safety. But it was useless. She could no more accept my graft than she could have accepted my tissue. Antibodies developed, and the graft withered and dropped without even transmitting any of the feelings to her. She was disappointed, and the antigen dose had the usual unpleasant effects, but she was spared the disturbance and the grief.

It could have been foreseen that this would happen, but there was just the chance of something different. All the same, it was very sad for Francoise, who had, I think, some slight feeling that this might have counted in some way against what she had done, so that we would at least think of her again as one of ourselves. I took care to thank her specially for what she had done, though Olga took it for granted—and that may have been the better way. I don't know. But all that was happening while I was still drifting, not conscious.

The other thing that happened was that Daisy gave birth not to eight half-mastiff puppies, but to eight dreadful little objects, each of which was like a slightly developed foetus swollen out with a graft-like texture. Poor Daisy hated them so much that she had an atavistic temptation to eat them. She succumbed to this and ate a couple; we all sympathised with her and managed to wipe out all the guilt feelings. The others were taken away, and everything was done to keep them alive; but they failed to ingest any food offered or to grow. In fact, they were a pretty thorough morphological and biochemical mess-up. Obviously the graft cycle had gone wrong here. But many of the Martian pseudo-toad eggs developed into small grafts which readily ingested bits of the plants out of their own world which Olga and Rima had grown for them. They put out pseudopodia and oozed about the place as though they were quite at home. I remember watching them among the bruised leaves, apparently perfectly at ease, and how Olga reflectively kicked one of them; she had taken against the grafts.

But that was later. What Zloin was saying to me when I got through to her was that her graft would have been different, would have been kind. (The meaning Zlion conveyed was not, of course, "kind", but a rather different Martian concept which cannot be translated exactly, to do with one's relations towards other beings.) It would have had various types of understanding. She had already perceived these. I asked why had she not told anyone? They would have come and interfered, measured, spoilt the secret between her and her graft. Why had she not told me, her friend? I would have betrayed her, I was a Terran too.

I tried to explain to her what now I could perceive, although through a veil of grief: that her graft, like mine, must fullfil its cycle, take us down into the water and as an entity, as the thing which had aroused love in us, cease to be. But Zloin refused to understand, channeled only hatred of Terrans. I could not communicate against that, partly because my own grief was still inhibiting my intelligence. But it was terrible, feeling her negating even the elementary solar loyalties which are common to all our childhoods. Now the dark dizziness was coming back on me, for they had given me a good knock-out dose of narcotic. I just remember murmuring for help to Peder, who lifted me off poor Zloin. Darkness and his arms wrapped me.

When I finally came to completely, the grief was almost gone, only a kind of bruise on the back of my mind. But I was very strongly filled with the feeling that I had behaved badly, that the tiny observer at the deep centre down the endless passage should not have allowed herself to be overwhelmed. Later I found just the same thing with my colleague Zloin, who was beginning to feel guilty and ashamed because she (or by now he) had hated Terrans and had allowed the feeling to escape. Zloin kept on telling me that whatever feelings had inadvertently come to the surface, I was different, not quite so Terran, more understanding. "You have drunk our wine," said Zloin.

I said that indeed I had, and spoke about Vly. "So it was you," Zloin said (I translate as closely as I can). "Where then is the child?"

I answered that Viola was doubtless with her friends, but she would be going to Mars soon. Zloin and I agreed almost too eagerly that these visitings to and fro were an excellent thing. We talked about Vly; she told me that his—or her—child had a beautifully marked skull. Suddenly I thought how much I would like to see Viola again before she left. When Peder came in I asked if he knew where she was.

"But, love," said Peder, "she started a month ago."

I looked at him stupidly. "But you," I said. "Haven't you gone?"

"You can see me," he said, and grinned. "I wasn't leaving you, Mary, the way you were."

I didn't know what to say. One doesn't expect an adult colleague to behave in this kind of way. Would I have done it myself for Peder? Suddenly I thought, well, perhaps I would. I began to say something, I didn't know what. He stopped me, swearing softly to himself; I remember he said: "It wasn't a difficult choice to make." He went on: "Did you know Viola was working on znydgi, the various colonies we have on Terra?" I shook my head. "I didn't think you knew," he said. "Possibly—she didn't want to tell you yet. I expect it was just an accident that she told me."

It was odd. I had felt the tiniest bit of resentment that she hadn't told me, and then I began laughing—but, of course, Peder was the obvious person to tell! But what in all the galaxies had she found? "Do go on!" I said .

"Well, it looks as if she's managed to live with the znydgi without getting cross with them—as I know you get, my love! Possibly it had to do with her size. She could go round among them and they didn't recognise her."

"They don't recognise anyone."

"That's what's said," Peder answered slowly, scratching his thick hair. "Yes, that's what we all say. But maybe it isn't true."

"Do you mean—"

"She didn't pay any attention to all that squealing which is neither here nor there. At least that's what she told me. It seems there's something else. And it's on her level. And they didn't think that she was anything to make them become stones." I was listening intently now, I saw what he meant—what Viola meant. I nodded. "Well, when she gets to their own planet she's going to find some that have never had any contact and watch. She has some ideas. But she isn't saying till she's sure."

"She's right there," I said. I suddenly thought, are the znydgi being stones to their grafts too? I went on. "But do you think she can possibly be going to make it? Really, Peder, really and truly? When neither the Martians nor ourselves have got anywhere?"

"Perhaps we might have if the Martians hadn't told us it was impossible. We reinforced one another. Anyhow, one day someone was bound to get the answer," Peder said. "Why not Viola? You've got the instinct for communication, Mary—I'm sorry to use a romantic old word like instinct, but it can still describe something—and when your genes are reinforced in her as they're bound to be without the normal chromosome partners—she might be the one, Mary."

"She'd make her name," I said. "Not that the znydgi are important, but it's been a thing we've all tried our hands on and failed. Oh, it would be fun! And if she managed any kind of contact there, think what she'd be like on some of our big problems! We'd all be shouting to get her on to our expeditions."

"You'd be pleased, Mary, wouldn't you?"

"Oh so pleased. I was afraid she might have to be time-bound. Oh Peder—" And then I remember I began to cry for no reason except that I was still weakened from the narcotics and the shock and because I still felt not entirely myself, not entirely stable. And Peder sat there like a mountain, a great, snow-peaked, unclimbed mountain of our own earth.

We stayed, of course, for the discussion. And, by the way, my eldest son turned up for it; I was pleased and rather flattered because he was just preparing for his first space voyage. But we'd been in the news. Silis, I noticed, found him very attractive. He listened in to all our problems. There was, for instance, the difficulty that the first grafts had deliquesced in water, but had not attacked or been attracted by (how near the two things are!) the ova or future ova of their hosts. We put it down simply to the loss of vitality among the earlier grafts who had suffered interruption of their life cycle so often. They did not, as it were, know what to do. In the symbiotic stage, they had last been with the Diners: their patterning was for maternal love and water. But, in the course of being cut up and regrown, they had lost the next phase. It seems probable that we shall soon find the molecular basis for this.

A lot of further work will have to be done. It will be essential, for instance, to discover how the grafts influence their female hosts, whether, for example, it is through some type of hormonic suppressor or encourager. It was certainly not a simple hormone reaction; our samples showed that. However, all the samples or tests must be completely evaluated. But this should not be too difficult.

All the same, I doubt if I want to be in on this one when the next grafting is done. Silis might take a turn now she is back.

It was on the last day of the discussion that someone brought a message to Pete. He hesitated a little, I remember, before letting us all know! It was about the escape of some of the psuedo-toad eggs, presumably down the drain from the pond. And the next thing, they matured and grew and as soon as the baby toads developed, they began going for the vegetable fields, having discovered some of their home flora. The centre was in real trouble with the police, not undeserved: violence had to be used on the toads, which was a bit upsetting and guilt-making. Luckily the hyaena was quite partial to toad flesh, and, as everyone felt rather guilty towards her, some balance was achieved. But it was alarming to think of how much delicious taste and texture could be destroyed by the toads, who didn't, one can be practically certain, enjoy it as such.

It was during the discussion that I had a good look at the very curious photographs which Pete had taken of me with my graft; it gave me peculiar residual feelings even now. Yes, I had been somebody else. Somebody, from a scientific point of view, delinquent. It had affected me more deeply this time than I had been affected earlier on in my contact with the radiates, the reason doubtless being that I had been involved not merely through my own curiosity and sympathy, but through an active and dangerous emotion generated from outside, even though I had been willing to accept it. But we are not yet able to prepare ourselves completely against such attacks, especially not if we are also communications experts, needing to keep all channels open.

I looked at the photographs again. Was that really me? Would my children recognise them? And was I yet sure whether I was back and normal? Intellectually perhaps. But not emotionally. "I shall have to stabilise before my next expedition," I said to Peder, leaning back against his shoulder, thinking about the daughter we had agreed to have.

We started for Trondhjem in an old-fashioned half-empty plane on a pale blue morning. Francoise was crying a little when she said goodbye. I think she envied me, perhaps for more reasons than one.